THE MOST DANGEROUS MAN

Also available by Jack Murphy

The Deckard Series

Gray Matter Splatter
Direct Action
Target Deck
Reflexive Fire

Nonfiction

We Defy: The Lost Chapters of Special Forces History
Murphy's Law: My Journey from Army Ranger and Green Beret to Investigative Journalist

THE MOST DANGEROUS MAN

A THRILLER

JACK MURPHY

CROOKED LANE

NEW YORK

Books should be disposed of and recycled according to local requirements. All paper materials used are FSC compliant.

This is a work of fiction. All of the names, characters, organizations, places, and events portrayed in this novel are either products of the author's imagination or are used fictitiously. Any resemblance to real or actual events, locales, or persons, living or dead, is entirely coincidental.

Published in the United States by Crooked Lane Books, an imprint of The Quick Brown Fox & Company LLC.

Crooked Lane Books and its logo are trademarks of The Quick Brown Fox & Company LLC.

Library of Congress Catalog-in-Publication data available upon request.

ISBN (hardcover): 979-8-89242-450-9
ISBN (paperback): 979-8-89242-451-6
ISBN (ebook): 979-8-89242-452-3

Cover design by Emily Mahar

Printed in the United States.

www.crookedlanebooks.com

Crooked Lane Books
34 West 27th St., 10th Floor
New York, NY 10001

First Edition: June 2026

The authorized representative in the EU for product safety and compliance is eucomply OÜPärnu mnt 139b-14, 11317 Tallinn, Estonia, hello@eucompliancepartner.com, +33757690241

10 9 8 7 6 5 4 3 2 1

For Kasiet

CHAPTER

1

A BOOTED FOOT SHOVED a metal folding chair, sending it skidding across the room, where it slapped against the drywall.

"Sit down right there."

Fluorescent bulbs hummed above the soldier as he walked into the small basement room and took a seat. A heavy metal door swung shut behind the men.

"This is an informal 15–6 investigation," one of the two military officers turned interrogators informed Lopez, the soldier in the chair. He knew that a 15–6 was a standard Army investigation and that if incriminating evidence was uncovered, it could lead to a court-martial.

He didn't know what an *informal* 15–6 was, though, and said as much.

"Informal means no sworn statements. Nothing on the record, no paper trail."

Lopez rubbed his forehead as the two officers grabbed their own folding chairs and sat down in front of him, ninety degrees from each other, surrounding him in an

L shape. Lopez hadn't slept in days, and network news was already reporting what had transpired over the last forty hours, which gave him some indication as to why the embassy was giving him the third degree.

One of the officers, wearing the rank of major, took off his uniform top and slung it over the back of his chair.

"Start at the beginning."

* * *

Deadfall and clipped pieces of brush were cast aside in the darkness, revealing a camouflage net concealing a Yamaha ATV four-wheeler. Lopez wore Mirage camo fatigue pants and a mesh ghillie suit top over his clothes. He was running late but proud of his work. He had spent hours creeping up on the terrorist compound, carefully placing large plastic "rocks" that contained high-tech surveillance equipment, including thermal and night vision cameras.

Opening his Toughbook computer, he dialed down the glow from the screen as he began syncing the cameras. Next, he began unfolding and connecting his satellite antenna and establishing the uplink. Both cameras were charged and functioning correctly.

He had hidden them in a manner that allowed the uplink to view different sides of the same building, getting as much coverage as possible. Human bodies showed up "white hot" on the screen, as did car engines. One carload had already arrived, and a second was pulling up as he watched the screen. It was five kilometers between him and the compound, but one could never be so sure of remaining hidden in this part of West Africa. No matter how careful you were, a shepherd or a cluster of children would stumble upon you sooner or later.

Pulling on a headset, he clicked the push-to-talk device attached to it.

"This is Romeo Three, radio check, over," he said.

"Romeo Three, this is X-Ray Zero-One, I read you. Status report on target?"

Lopez recognized the call sign as belonging to one of the A Squadron leaders of the Delta Force element that was currently operating under the code name Gabled Stone, which was now en route on MH-60 helicopters flown by the 160th Special Operations Aviation Regiment, also known as the Nightstalkers.

"I've got two vehicles on the white side of the objective," he replied, referring to the side of the compound that would be facing the assaulters as they disembarked from the aircraft. Each of the four sides of the compound was color-coded white, black, green, or red. "Counted a total of five military-aged males entering, over."

The transmission turned to static for a moment. The operators were already in the air.

"Roger that, Romeo Three, keep us updated. We are approximately thirty mikes to TOT, out."

Thirty minutes until the helicopters landed, or time on target.

He continued to monitor the camera feeds, counting three more vehicles over the next twenty-five minutes and calling them out on the assault net for the Delta operators to hear. The newcomers were not unexpected; intel had indicated that the bad guys were getting together for some kind of powwow, which made it a high-percentage target for Delta. It was an opportunity to wrap up the whole network in one raid.

"Five minutes," he heard a new voice announce on the assault net.

Lopez used the zoom feature on the cameras to call out the positions of several sentries outside the compound, and one guy sitting on a car hood who looked to be smoking a cigarette.

"One minute." The transmission sounding garbled over the roar of the MH-60 Black Hawk's rotor blades.

He could just barely make out the *thump-thump-thump* of the rotors in the distance, and only because he was listening for them.

"Thirty seconds."

WHOOOSH.

He nearly jumped out of his skin at the sound coming from his right flank. It was distinctly not the sound of a helicopter but something on the ground.

Craning his neck, Lopez saw a fireball illuminate the night sky, the glow momentarily reflecting on his face. It could only be the result of a surface-to-air missile.

"Mayday, Mayday, Mayday!" someone screamed over the net.

The fireball descended to the ground, and he heard a thud off in the distance. It was difficult to estimate range at night, but he figured the crash to be about four kilometers out.

The assault net was buzzing. It was too late for the other helicopters to peel off the target; they were already flaring and landing. On the screen, he could see the operators dashing across the Sahel, some carrying ladders or breaching equipment. Their suppressed Sig Sauer rifles made short work of the sentries. It took only a second for them to affix the breaching charge. His computer screen went white hot for a moment when the charge blew. The entire troop then began flowing into and flooding the compound with operators.

"This is Romeo Three, coming off station," Lopez announced. His part of the job, the reconnaissance, was finished, but he wasn't going to sit on his ass while Americans were on the ground at the crash site. "Moving to the area of the crash site."

"Roger," came the reply over the assault net.

Slamming the computer shut and folding up the antenna, he packed up the whole ball of cables and electronics into a pouch on the side of the ATV, slung his M110A1 rifle over his back, and started the engine. He backed out of his improvised hide site in the bushes, nosed toward where he expected to find the crash site, then gunned the engine.

They had a Black Hawk down.

* * *

"Hold up, let me get this straight," the major blurted. "You unilaterally decided to come off your station and move to the crash site?"

"I announced it over the assault net and got a confirmation."

"We just spent twelve hours in an after-action review with the Delta guys, and no one remembers acknowledging your decision."

"Well, pull the tapes."

"We're still waiting on those, and you sure as shit better hope that your story holds up, because the command is calling bullshit. What call sign acknowledged you?"

"I don't know; they didn't give a call sign. There was a lot of frantic traffic on the assault net after that bird went down."

"If they didn't acknowledge you by call sign or give their own, how do you even know they were talking to you?"

"Should I have a lawyer present for this shit?"

"Let's get back on track," the second officer, a captain, interrupted.

* * *

The ATV tore across the Sahel, the wind rushing through his hair as he struggled to see what was in front of him through the dual-tube PVS-31A night vision goggles he wore, as he could see only so far without stopping to readjust the focus on the tubes. Between the dust in the air and the overcast night, Lopez couldn't see shit, so he risked flipping on his white lights, pushing the night vision up and out of his face on its pivot mount.

Up ahead he saw the glow of what had to be a downed MH-60, which was the Special Operations variant of the UH-60 Black Hawk helicopter that most of the Army used. The MH-60 was flown by the Nightstalkers, the 160th Special Operations Aviation Regiment, and the new MH-60M model was packed with high-tech optical equipment, electronic countermeasures, and an advanced radar system in addition to the pod that jutted out in front of the cockpit for midair refueling.

With nothing left between him and the crash but occasional trees and shrubs, he gunned the throttle again and sped forward, hoping to get to the crash site before any hostiles arrived. Seconds seemed like minutes, which seemed like hours, the passage of time distorted by the unique time dilation effect that combat has on the human mind.

Finally, he spotted the crash ahead. The MH-60 was lying upside down, exposing its belly to the night sky. The rotor blades appeared to have been sheared off during the crash. A Black Hawk down in this part of the world had an ominous history, going back to Operation Gothic Serpent in Somalia over thirty years ago, that didn't bode well for the soldier and his unit. Two forms moved around the wreckage.

Unslinging his M110A1 rifle, he flipped on the night vision attachment to his 10x scope. In years past he would have used an IR laser to shoot at night, but night vision devices had proliferated among terrorist organizations over the last decade. An infrared beam could give away your position and telegraph your attack if the enemy had night vision.

Through his sniper scope, he saw that the two forms around the wreckage wore baggy clothes and head coverings and carried Kalashnikov rifles. He clenched his hand on his pistol grip and rotated the safety catch from safe to semi as he leaned forward in the seat of the ATV and used the handlebars to help stabilize his firing position. The rules of engagement on this op were not totally clear, but no one would argue if he was taking action to protect a downed flight crew from terrorists.

He gently stroked the trigger, putting down the first target with a 7.62mm round to the chest before slightly rotating his upper body to transition to the second target and squeezing the trigger again. Both terrorists were down with less than a second between shots.

Lopez took no pleasure in the act, nor did he feel bad about it. Killing was part of the job, and it was just business to him, not something personal. At the moment, those terrorists were between him and the flight crew, and getting to his comrades and keeping them alive was the priority. In the process of accomplishing that, the new enemy had to die. It was what it was.

After a quick scan for any additional enemy, he slung the rifle, then rode the ATV forward the last fifty meters and circled the wreck.

Shutting down the ATV, he climbed down and inspected the wreckage. The fuselage was intact; the pilot had clearly made a semicontrolled crash landing as opposed to just falling out of the sky. He didn't see any clear sign of a surface-to-air missile strike, but it might have taken off one of the rotor blades; that would have been enough to bring the bird down. Peering inside the cockpit, he saw that both pilots had unstrapped their safety belts and reached for weapons before they were both executed at point-blank range. The entry wounds were clear enough.

But he also knew from his time in Afghanistan that an MH-60 should have two pilots and two crew members who would have manned the side-mounted miniguns. Neither crew member was at the crash site.

Making another lap around the wreckage, he found footprints in the sand. Footprints and expended brass. As he crept forward, he found both 5.56 brass and 7.62×39 brass, indicating that the crew members had clearly survived and engaged the enemy in a close-range firefight. The footprints trailed off into the darkness. Not more than fifteen minutes had elapsed since the crash. They couldn't have gone far.

Without radio contact with the survivors, this was going to be super sketch.

He held his rifle at the low ready, and began to pursue. He was leaving behind the two pilots. The Ranger Creed clearly stated, "Never shall I leave a fallen comrade." It was what they had to fall back on in times like this. But he also knew that if he had a chance to help rescue the crew members, the pilots would have supported his decision. The Army would be back for the pilot's remains regardless. They would not be abandoned.

It was a difficult decision to make, even if it was the right one.

Man-tracking at night was notoriously difficult, some said impossible, but he did have a few techniques up his sleeve. One of them was breaking the rules about the use of IR that the enemy might be able to see.

Crouching down, he turned on the infrared flashlight on his rifle and swept his barrel back and forth across the Sahel while scanning with his night vision goggles down. The IR flashlight created nonvisible light that could be seen only with night vision, and through the goggles, that light cast shadows inside footprints on the ground.

Picking up the spoor again, he began forward, increasing his pace as he heard gunfire in the distance. It sounded to be about two hundred meters ahead of him, in his direction of travel. He moved as quickly and as quietly as possible. Soon, he began seeing muzzle flashes. They lit up the night like strobe lights. Knowing he was about to stumble upon both enemies and friendlies (who didn't know who he was), he began using the trees for cover, darting from one to the other as he made his way forward.

Up ahead was a copse of trees sticking up out of the thorny brush that was scattered across the Sahel. A muzzle flash emanated from somewhere within. Two more replied from his right flank, sounding like Kalashnikovs. Again using the night sight on his rifle, he scanned and picked up the two muzzle flashes in the distance. They were under the trees, and it was an overcast night—impossible to confirm if they were friendly or enemy, although he had some intuition that the helicopter crew were in the bushes and these were the bad guys.

Lopez began creeping forward toward the copse of trees as the firefight continued, like a staccato conversation held in gunfire, each communication a potentially deadly reply.

Within thirty meters he yelled into the trees, "*Ranger! Ranger!* Friendly coming in!"

There was a pause, then more gunfire.

"*Ranger! Ranger!*" he repeated.

Fuck.

He continued creeping forward until he saw a silhouette crouched in the bushes, the muzzle of his rifle pointing toward the trees, where the two terrorists appeared to be moving to outflank him.

"*Ranger!*" he yelled from less than ten meters behind the form, but he still received no response, his words drowned out by the gunfire.

"Fine, fuck it," he said under his breath.

The reconnaissance expert did what he did best, what he had done on dozens of close-target recce missions around the world. He crept right up on someone without them knowing he was there. His Salomon trail runners were silent on the desert sand as he stepped from heel to toe. The gunman in front of him was still returning fire, and the two bad guys still appeared to be on the move.

"Hey, bud," he said, putting his hand on the gunman's shoulder, causing him to nearly jump out of his skin. The man was wearing a flight suit and firing an M4 rifle. He must be one of the crew members, but now he was scared and swinging his rifle muzzle toward Lopez. Reaching down, Lopez pushed the muzzle away and said again, "Ranger!"

The crew member's eyes were as wide as saucers.

"What? You're American?"

"Yeah, man."

"Who are you? We weren't briefed on any Rangers being out here." The crew member looked him up and down, noting the strange camo pattern on his fatigues that he had never seen before. Some sort of digital pattern with all kinds of different colors in it.

"You got briefed on Romeo Three doing the recon for the mission?"

"Yeah, the recce team."

"Well, it turned out to be just me. I'm with the Regimental Reconnaissance Company, Team Three."

The crew member blinked.

"What is that?"

* * *

"Yeah, same question," the captain said. "What the fuck is RRC, and how did they wind up on this mission?"

"Well, they didn't. I did because I was detached from Team Three to do some recce work in Niger."

"What kind of recce work?"

"You'd have to ask the Ranger Regiment that question. It's read-on only."

"You're telling me that we don't have a need to know?" the captain asked.

"You're addressing a commissioned officer in the United States Army, Sergeant," the major dutifully reminded Lopez. "You will address us as *sir* and show proper decorum."

"RRC is a little-known recon element that is a part of the 75th Ranger Regiment, but often JSOC has operational control over our taskings. I got pulled off my mission here when Delta got a 0300 counterterrorism alert for rapid deployment as intel developed on a target they had been keeping an eye on. They found out I was here and tasked me to help with the recce portion of the mission."

"Sir," the Major reminded him.

"Sir."

"RRC consists of just six six-man recon teams, so there are only thirty-six of us at best, plus a few commo guys, all source intelligence analysts and so on, which is why most people haven't heard of us."

"All right, whatever we're moving on . . ."

* * *

"Never mind, I think we got bigger problems," Lopez said as the sound of dirt bikes echoed nearby. The enemy was about to swarm in on the sounds of the firefight, and he could already hear the bark of Kalashnikov fire getting closer. "There is another one of you?"

"He didn't make it," the crew member said, gesturing to what initially looked like a part of the bushes under night vision. Lopez moved forward, and checking for a pulse confirmed that the other crew member was deceased.

Lopez, propped his inner elbow on his knee as he looked through the scope. Three dirt bikes had broken from the cover of the trees and were screaming down on their position. He squeezed the trigger, his round taking the lead rider just below the neck and sending him tumbling backward off the bike.

Oddly, the dirt bike continued to remain upright, and with the engine still running, it careened out of Lopez's field of vision.

It took two shots to bring down the second dirt bike–riding terrorist, sending both the bike and the rider sideways in a cloud of dust. The third rider hesitated, realizing he was now alone with the Americans directly to his front. That split second cost him, and he took a long dirt nap courtesy of the RRC Ranger.

Back at the tree line, the situation was quickly deteriorating. Two technicals, Toyota Hilux pickup trucks with DShK machine guns mounted in the back, pulled up and disgorged a dozen more terrorists.

"You got comms up?"

"Survival radio only," the crew member reported. "The CAG element is being rerouted to our location. Should be a few minutes out."

We might not have a few minutes, Lopez thought to himself.

"Let them know that I'm colocated with you."

"What was your call sign again?"

"Romeo Three, last name Lopez."

"Roger," the 160th crew member said as he began speaking into his radio.

Lopez extended his bipod legs and looked down his scope as the technicals and dismounts began to shake out into an assault line that would sweep forward toward their location in mere moments.

The dull thump of the rotors could already be heard in the distance.

"Are we gonna make it?" the crew member asked, the first sign of fear creeping into his voice.

"We just need to hold out until those birds get here. All I can do is slow the bad guys down a little, maybe buy us some time."

A trained sniper, Lopez quickly assessed his priority of targets. First, the machine gunners in the back of the two technicals, who manned the enemy's greatest casualty-producing weapons. Then the drivers; taking them out would render the vehicles at least temporarily immobile. Then he could sweep up the ash and trash.

For all his training, weapons, and equipment, their survival looked to hinge on a single dice roll. Either they would take down enough enemy and hold out and survive before reinforcements arrived, or they wouldn't.

Lopez rotated the selector switch on his rifle from safe to semi.

* * *

"So it was a real roll of the dice, but the other 160th Black Hawks showed up at the last moment. I was almost out of ammo when suddenly the door gunners opened up with miniguns."

The two officers looked at each other.

"You made a series of highly questionable tactical decisions," the major said.

"But I made them," Lopez replied. "Any decision is better than no decision. I was on my own and reacted as quickly as I could to save as many teammates as I could."

The major frowned. They were at an impasse. If the two officers couldn't dig up some dirt on him or get him to compromise himself somehow, then the investigation would quickly be dropped, and instead of calling a court-martial they would be pinning a medal on Lopez for valor under fire. It was a hero-or-zero moment, and the three of them damn well knew it.

"Jeremy Lopez," the major said with contempt in his voice. "What do they call you for short? J-Lo?"

The officers broke out laughing.

"Yes, sir," Lopez replied.

They stopped laughing.

"Seriously?"

"Listen, fellas, it's only in the movies where soldiers get nicknames like Deathbringer or Death Dealer or whatever. In Ranger battalion, you're going to get a nickname like Ballduster or Cock Face or, in my case, J-Lo."

"That accent," the captain said. "I take it you're from the south. Tennessee or Alabama?"

"Alabama."

"You joined the Army right out of the Redneck Riviera, didn't you, Sergeant?"

"I'll have you know that my cultural heritage constitutes a part of the rich tapestry of our great nation, *sir.*"

The major exploded out of his chair and flung a finger toward the door.

"Get the fuck out of here!"

CHAPTER 2

THE HUNTER HEARD a rustling in the bushes and gently trained the barrel of his rifle in that direction. He squinted hard against the sweat streaming down his face as he stared through the 10x scope, trying to spot his quarry off in the distance across the Savanna.

"Easy," his Safari guide cautioned in his South African–accented English. "Don't rush it."

The hunter was tech entrepreneur Lucas Ramachandran, who, although he was an immigrant from India, reflected on the reality that he was a far ways away from Silicon Valley. In fact, he was in West Africa doing something very illegal that he could never get away with back in the States.

He braced the rifle in the crossbar created by two plastic sticks, made specifically for hunters in environments like this where the grass was waist height. The sticks allowed him to fire over the grass while also in a more stable supported firing position.

The South African leaned in, nearly whispering in his ear.

"Right there, through the trees," he said. "You see the movement."

Lucas blinked sweat out of his eyes. Through the foliage, he did indeed see what looked like something moving laterally. But what was it? There were gazelles, lions, even elephants out here. Big game to be sure, but was it the right game?

The South African, a grizzled veteran hunter named Koos DeKlerk, had worked with Lucas, helping him stalk through the forest and savanna and gain a firing position that had taken the better part of the day to achieve. The safari guide seemed to know the national park like the back of his hand.

"I see it," Lucas confirmed.

"That's your trophy right there, boet," the South African whispered. "The only thing left is for you to take the shot. Like I said, do not rush it."

Lucas nodded slightly, both tension and anticipation building in his body. His hand was a little shaky as he carefully rested his finger on the trigger. He saw the movement again now, clearly, through breaks between the tree branches and leaves. As he aimed his cross hairs center mass on the target, his finger began taking up the slack in the trigger.

"Easy goes it," the South African coaxed him.

The shot caught Lucas by surprise when the trigger finally broke. The round blasted downrange, and Lucas nearly jumped out of his skin. His sudden movement sent both the rifle and the shooting sticks tumbling to the ground. The Indian American was beyond mortified to have embarrassed himself in front of the seasoned guide and began collecting the rifle before even looking downrange.

But DeKlerk was already scanning ahead with his binoculars.

"You tagged him, but let's confirm the kill," he announced.

Lucas eyes went wide. He was ecstatic with the news. Grabbing up the sticks, he slung the rifle, and the two of them marched forward through the high grass. As they grew near, DeKlerk unslung his own rifle and began moving forward carefully.

As he had told Lucas earlier, the most dangerous part of a hunt was during the follow-up. You might have injured the beast, and now you had him cornered. That was when he'd fight back the hardest.

As the branches separated with their passage, the two hunters could see a prostrate form lying in the grass beyond. Now Lucas couldn't contain himself; he broke through the brush and ran toward his trophy.

He rushed over, kicked the body to make sure it was dead, and then he flipped it over to examine it.

"Well done, lad," DeKlerk said as he pulled a digital camera from his pack. "Well done."

Lucas reached down, grabbed the African's head by the ears, and lifted him up, posing with the human corpse for a trophy photo. DeKlerk took a half dozen photos to commemorate the event. A rusty bolt-action Mosin-Nagant rifle lay next to the dead African. He had been a poacher on the national reserve, illegally hunting elephants to sell their ivory on the black market. No one was going to miss him.

The tech bro smiled a toothy smile as the shutter on the digital camera clicked again and again.

It had been a convoluted journey for the young man, from first-generation immigrant to idealistic hustler in Silicon Valley to where he was now. It was actually the failed liberal policies of San Francisco that had led to his political awakening, and then to his spiral down conspiracy theory rabbit holes, ethnonationalism, and reactionary politics.

As he tuned out the mainstream media propaganda, he found an odd form of comfort in trolling 4chan and Reddit, where his views grew only more extreme. His racism melded with the desire to be different and edgy, to do things that were transgressive and unpermitted by "normies." He found exactly what he was looking for in a group of like-minded Silicon tech bros.

For a few years he had heard rumors about the hunts. Only rumors. It was only a few weeks ago that he was finally invited on one.

"Let's bring up the truck," DeKlerk said, "and get your kill back to the camp."

Backtracking straight to the vehicle was much faster than the stalk itself, and they were soon inside the rusty pickup truck and barreling through the dry, straw-colored grass. Once they arrived at the site of the kill, Lucas took the poacher's corpse by the ankles while DeKlerk hooked his hands under the arms. They carried him around the truck and flopped him down on the open tailgate.

The South African rolled the corpse forward and slammed the tailgate shut. He patted the side of the truck, a small acknowledgment to himself for a hard day's work complete. A few hours later they arrived at their base camp.

In a large clearing between the trees, a number of tents had been erected. As they parked and exited the truck, a generator could be heard purring gently on the outskirts of the camp.

"So did he bust his cherry?" someone asked almost the moment they came into the camp. The hunting party began emerging from their tents and surrounding the pickup truck.

DeKlerk dropped the tailgate on the truck.

"We have a kill," he announced.

The nine hunters and one safari guide gathered around the back of the truck while Lucas climbed up and began dragging the dead body by the wrists.

Several of the hunters cheered as the body was splayed out on the tailgate.

"Outstanding work, Lucas," one of the hunters said.

"About time," another muttered. "Can we get on with the main event now?"

DeKlerk smiled and reached for the satellite phone in his pack.

"Indeed we can."

Punching a number into the keypad, he held the phone to his ear while it rang.

* * *

It had been nearly forty-eight hours since the crash when staff sergeant Jeremy Lopez finally left the US embassy in Niamey, Niger. Pushing through the glass door, he emerged into the blazing heat of the afternoon. The embassy itself was designed to look quite modern, with sand-colored walls and red metal planking going up some of them. The color scheme of sand, stone, and red oxide was clearly an attempt to mimic the local structures.

The new embassy had been built only a few years ago, and while relatively small, it became a hub for US government personnel every time something popped off in the region.

Lopez had endured round after round of after-action Joint Special Operations Command reviews that eventually started to feel like interrogations. Being a recon Ranger made him a redheaded stepchild within JSOC at times, never mind his many deployments to Afghanistan on Omega teams and ops in West and East Africa and Syria.

He was assigned to Regimental Reconnaissance Company Team Three, but RRC was "one up" in Niger, meaning he was the lone Ranger there at the moment. Out of the six-man team, they had one guy in Northwest Syria, two in Somalia working on the Puntland Strike Force deal, two more in Yemen working another recon job, and then him in Niger.

They trained together as a team and sometimes deployed as a six-man element, but getting deployed in onesies and twosies seemed to have become more common in recent years. JSOC was getting big into so-called "blended teams" that merged the capabilities of different special ops units. For instance, a small special ops task force in a country might have a Delta Force team leader, an RRC assistant team leader, and a few Task Force Orange signals intelligence guys and that was it.

Lopez had done a few pumps like that in parts of the Middle East and Africa in recent years.

Anyway, a simple thank-you from JSOC for a job well done would have sufficed. Not that he didn't appreciate the miniguns on the additional 160th helicopters pulling his ass out of the fire.

On CNN, the Pentagon was claiming that one of their helicopters had experienced a mechanical malfunction during an operation in Niger and had a "hard landing," which was typical US military obfuscation, especially when something embarrassing had happened.

Well, fuck it.

Lopez knew of a local watering hole where he could drown out some of the administrative stress and combat fatigue. He'd been in the Ranger Regiment for close to ten years and in RRC for five or so. He had little patience for bellicose pussies wearing officer rank.

Out in the embassy parking lot, he squinted against the glare of a slowly descending sun. Across the way he saw someone he recognized, wearing what was sometimes known in the profession as a 5.11 tuxedo. Tan cargo pants, T-shirt, and ball cap completed a fashion choice that could be described as "business tactical."

"Hey, bro, what's up?" Lopez said as he neared.

The soldier turned toward him, his face also covered in several days of scruff, his eyes bloodshot and tired, likely from having endured a similar post-mission interrogation. His name was Eric Willoughby, but everyone just called him Wallaby. He was a seasoned operator for Task Force Orange, the Army intelligence unit known for a series of constantly changing code names, one of the most recent being Titan Zeus, TZ for short.

They were both recon specialists, in a sense, but had different roles in Niger. Lopez was there to handle the tactical side—reconning the actual objective, getting eyes on the bad guys, emplacing devices that could do the same. Wallaby's job was more in backside logistics; he had to scout out the airfield and potential helicopter landing zones for the Delta Force element before they arrived in-country.

It was one of those easily missed but critically important jobs in the special ops community. Wallaby spent long days and nights driving roads to do route reconnaissance, setting up safe houses, and liaising with the local military.

"Hey, Lopez," the weary Army spy said after a delayed recognition. He was tired, and the Ranger couldn't blame him; so was he. "Heard you got into a dustup out there."

"That's the *too long, didn't read* version, yeah."

"They interrogated me about the whole thing after the debriefing. Don't worry, bro, I put in a good word for you. Don't know why they have such a case of the ass with you."

"JSOC had a bird go down and some soldiers killed. They need to find someone to blame, and it sure as fuck is not going to be a commissioned officer."

"That's a no-shitter."

"I'm heading out for a drink. Want one?"

Wallaby chuckled. "No thanks, man, I'm exhausted. Got a few more things to do, and then I'm headed straight to my bunk."

"Suit yourself," Lopez said defiantly.

Wallaby laughed again. "See ya tomorrow, Ranger."

Lopez climbed into his assigned vehicle, a Land Cruiser, and drove out of the embassy gate and headed to the bar on the other side of town. He hadn't had much, if any, sleep, but *work hard, play hard* was a thing in the Ranger Regiment, and the Zaxi rooftop lounge and bar wasn't far at all. He cruised down the dusty paved streets, where the lanes were often divided by a median colored in red and white stripes like a candy cane.

He wore jeans, a black collared shirt, and a Glock 19, concealed inside his waistband holster, that he was permitted to carry under a status of forces agreement the United States had hashed out with the local government. The civilian attire was because he was supposed to be keeping a low profile, not only to avoid being targeted by the bad guys but also so he wouldn't irritate the populace, never mind the local security forces if possible.

The US military was in Niger by invitation of the local government, who wanted Uncle Sam's capabilities (read: money) to help counter "violent extremist groups," meaning the Islamic terror organizations plaguing the more rural parts of the country. To that end, a fairly robust special ops presence could be found at the US embassy and various Nigerien military bases dotted around the Sahel.

Special Forces, or Green Berets, did most of the hearts-and-minds village stability operations and key leader engagements. JSOC, Delta, and DEVGRU got called in when some heavy lifting needed to be done. One of the priorities was rescuing a number of American missionaries that the extremists were holding. With the Green Berets paving the way, Delta had been able to snatch one of the hostages out of a camp just a month ago.

The success of that mission was what had gotten Congress more interested in Niger, hence a recon specialist like Lopez getting deployed there.

A lot of internationals hung out at the Raddison hotel, and another white dude didn't attract any special attention. Technically, he was only half white, but it didn't make much difference in West Africa. He stood out like a sore thumb.

Finding himself a seat at the bar, he ordered a Scotch on the rocks. He was on his second drink and already nursing a shitty attitude about life when an absolute bombshell sat down next to him and ordered a Manhattan.

She made some casual comment about what he was drinking, and they flowed right into conversation. He noticed how slick her introduction had been, whatever she had said to break the ice, though he couldn't even remember what it had been and didn't care.

Maybe it was stress or sleep deprivation, but Lopez was a little starstruck. She had platinum-blonde hair and sky-blue eyes.

But more striking were her bedroom eyes and liquid smile.

"Cassandra," she said, holding out her hand.

Lopez took it gently. "Jeremy."

"What brings you out to Niamey?" she said, smiling.

"Contract gig at the embassy," he lied, feeding her a cover story to protect the operational security around why he was really there. "They brought me in to do a security assessment—you know, barbed wire, CCTV cameras, that type of thing."

"Sounds fun."

"Sounds like a drag, actually. What do you do out here?" he said, changing the subject.

"I'm with an NGO," she said referring to one of the nongovernmental organizations operating in Niger. "I guess you could say I do assessments as well, but we're mostly digging wells. We do a lot of health assessments on the villages and make recommendations to the government about how to improve conditions."

"Folks here need it. The conditions outside the city are pretty austere," Jeremy replied.

As they continued to talk, she ordered him a third drink, and he soon noticed that she kept leaning closer and closer. She was smiling a lot. She was laughing at his dumb jokes. She kept asking him to tell her his stupid stories about his upbringing or getting into trouble in third-world countries.

As he sipped his Scotch, Jeremy began to feel like Lady Luck was swinging back in his favor. Fuck the embassy and all their bullshit.

Then things began to get wobbly. The next thing he knew, he was in the bathroom taking a piss, then suddenly he was back at the bar with Cassandra. She was still peppering him with questions and being flirty.

"So, yeah, my grandpa grew up at the head of a holler," he was explaining.

"A what?"

"Like a valley. My grandparents dynamited their way into it and never left."

"One of your Americanisms," she said, flashing another smile. "I grew up in South Africa."

Jeremy blinked. He was feeling way drunker than he should.

Time passed, and he was telling yet another story.

"So, Jessica, the girl I was dating at the time, confronted me and says that I don't love anyone or anything. That I'm incapable of love. I told her that's not true. I love Batman. I love Boba Fett. Sadly, our relationship fell apart after that."

The next thing he knew, he was relating a story about being drunk at a bar in Atlanta and getting kicked out by bouncers. She was still smiling, still laughing, even as the walls began to close in on Jeremy.

He continued to hear his voice as he spoke, but it felt disembodied, as if he were hearing someone else speaking while everything grew darker.

Then he was pitched face-first into blackness, and Cassandra disappeared from his life.

CHAPTER

3

When Lopez began to wake up, he didn't remember much, but he knew he was in a place he was unfamiliar with. He reached out with his senses, trying to understand where he was, but his brain only came back to him with fog. Wherever he was, it was dark, damp, and cold. His forehead was pounding. That was all he knew.

An unknown amount of time passed before he was able to pry his eyes open and look around. He was in a large rectangular room with cement walls. Obnoxiously bright LED lights stung his eyes. Trying to clear the fog, he pushed up to his knees, his hands on the cool concrete floor.

On the other side of the room was a door. A large, rusty, metal door with no knob or locking mechanism on his side. That's when it hit him.

I'm fucked. They got me.

The big question was, who was *they*? Depending on which Islamic terror organization had captured him, he could look forward to either an orange jumpsuit and a beheading or a prolonged period of negotiation and release once a ransom was paid. On paper, the US government did not negotiate with terrorists, but there were exceptions built into that rule. They could pay a ransom if the intelligence community could track where the money went and use that information against the bad guys.

Of course, there was the possibility of the US military sending a rescue team, but how would they even know where he was being held? He imagined that back at the embassy he would be assessed as absent without leave, and people would only start to worry in another day or two.

But if he had been captured by terrorists, wouldn't they have killed him outright? Why put him in a cell instead of making a propaganda film where he got his head sawed off? Dozens of possibilities quickly ran through his mind before he gave up on what he realized was a self-torture session.

Lopez was a graduate of the Army's Survival, Evasion, Resistance, and Escape, or SERE, school, where soldiers learned how to resist interrogation and escape imprisonment. He'd even gone to the secret squirrel SERE course known as SERE 127, in which he was kidnapped from a hotel and wasn't told he was in an exercise until day three of captivity. He'd also gotten sent to the urban evasion course in Spokane, Washington, where he spent five days in a white jumpsuit eating out of garbage cans while conducting an urban escape and evasion.

What that experience had taught him was how important it was to maintain your own psychological profile. Let thoughts of failure or death into your mind, and you were finished in a situation like this. More information would come when it came. He would think. Bide his time. Plan.

Looking around his cell, he noticed it was barren—aside from one curiosity. In the corner of the cell was a small gym. It was ramshackle and decrepit but still a gym, which was unusual for a prison cell. As he stutter-stepped toward it, it dawned on Lopez for the first time that the reason he felt like he was moving in slow motion was because he had been drugged.

By that bitch in Niamey.

In the corner of the cell were a few dozen rusty old dumbbells, a couple of kettlebells, and an improvised barbell made out of a length of pipe and two coffee cans that had been filled with concrete. Maybe this room only doubled as a cell and was usually used for a gym? That would mean he would be held here for only a short period before being moved to another location, he speculated. Or his captors were really concerned about his physical fitness. They could have provided some protein shakes and pre-workout powder, he thought, shaking his head.

He jumped at the clang of metal on metal, like a steel shank being flung open. A slit opened in the bottom of his cell door, and a tray of food was dropped inside before the shank was slammed shut again.

Lopez looked down at his prison meal.

Another data point. Even in the cell, every new thing was a shred of information that told him something.

The tray was heaped with grilled meat and vegetables. There was also a bottle of water. The label said it was from a Swiss-based company, but that didn't mean anything, as

Lopez knew they were a massive company that sold products all over the world, including in West Africa. It was the quality of the food that surprised him. This wasn't prison grub or gruel intended to keep him weak but alive.

A prison cell with decent catering and a personal gym?

What the fuck is this?

CHAPTER

4

IT WAS IMPOSSIBLE to gauge the passage of time in the windowless prison cell. None of his data points were coming from the natural world outside. He had been thoroughly searched and left wearing just a T-shirt, jeans, and sneakers. His Par Weber watch was gone; his Glock was, of course, long gone too. They had even found the numerous holdouts he had hidden in his clothes, his belt, even his shoelaces, which had contained handcuff keys and various cutting devices to escape restraints.

Whoever searched him knew what they were doing. Another data point.

After finishing his meal and downing the entire bottle of water, Lopez was feeling better but still wanted to clear his head. He got to work in the small gym. It wasn't ideal, but workable. Even a lighter dumbbell or kettlebell could kick your ass after enough repetitions.

He warmed up with some man-makers with thirty-pound dumbbells. In the pushup position, he grasped both dumbbells and rowed each, one at a time, then sprang to his feet, executed a squat, and pressed both dumbbells over his head. That made one repetition of the exercise.

He continued on like that for some time, moving from man-makers to goblet squats to kettlebell swings. Suddenly, it was possible to judge the passage of time. For someone who exercised at max effort on a near daily basis, the tension, the exhaustion of his muscles, and his struggle to catch his breath all told him he had been working out for nearly an hour.

Taking an additional hour or so to cool down, he next busied himself by looking for materials to use to create improvised blades, or shanks. Using his time to improve his situation, even in nearly microscopic ways, was preferable to sitting around stewing in anxiety. Eventually he did find a few small pieces of metal that he was able to put into his pockets. He kept busy by running them across the concrete floor to sharpen them, until someone decided it was lights out.

The cell was plunged into darkness to the point that he couldn't see his hand right in front of his face. With no other real choice, he lay down and tried to sleep.

It went on like that for a while. Lopez kept count, couldn't be sure of the days, but he was given three periods of darkness when the lights were turned off. When the lights came back on, he was fed three square meals a day through the slot in the door. He placed himself in front of the door a few times to try to catch a glimpse of someone through the slot but never saw anything more than flickering shadows.

Lopez kept his body mobile and energized by using the gym and did his best to keep his mind occupied with thoughts of escape. He moved the weights around twice a day, carrying kettlebells across the cell, pressing them overhead, curling the ghetto coffee can barbell, whatever it took to keep himself occupied.

Then there was a fourth period of darkness. Lopez was trying to sleep on the cement floor when the prison door suddenly burst open. Pushing himself up on an elbow, Lopez squinted at the backlit man-sized silhouette standing in the doorway. The person wore a wide-brimmed hat, and Lopez immediately recognized his posture. He was holding a rifle, trained dead on him.

The Ranger was beginning to sit up when he felt something sharp thwack into his left pectoral muscle. Looking down, he saw a red-feathered stabilizer sticking out from the back of a small metal shaft that was now poking out of his chest.

A tranquilizer dart.

And it must have been some good shit, because it put him down and out before he could formulate another thought.

CHAPTER 5

LOPEZ HAD SOME vague notion of movement. His senses were wanting to turn back on but couldn't. Over and over again, he slipped back into blackness. At some point he began to hear things, and somewhere in the back of his mind he identified what sounded like a large fan at first, but eventually his foggy mind concluded that it was the prop of an airplane whirling.

Slowly, he began to see daylight. His eyes opened.

He was in a clearing in a forested area; he could tell that much. A small prop plane had landed there and now sat idle. Focusing was a struggle, as whatever he had been tranquilized with was clouding his head. The pounding headache quickly evolved into the all-too-familiar beating of a helicopter's rotor blades in the distance. Minutes later, they became a reality when a white-and-blue helicopter landed in the clearing.

Lopez could see the doors opening and people disembarking, but it was a struggle to keep his eyes open. He faded back out.

"So this is him?"

It was some time later. Lopez opened his eyes and fought against the sting of the sunlight. A bottle of water rolled next to him.

"I've kept him in fine fighting condition until you arrived," someone else said in accented English.

"Doesn't look like much."

"He's still waking up. I put enough tranquilizer into him to put down a horse. Didn't want him waking up and causing a scene on the way here."

Lopez rolled over onto his back and stared up at a bunch of white faces. He counted eight of them altogether. He sat up as his mind began to clear. The gaggle of people had surrounded him. They wore a combination of high-end outdoor clothing and military gear.

What the hell is going on here? These guys look like they're getting ready for a paintball game, Lopez thought.

The next thing he noticed was the manacle around his left ankle, which was attached to a heavy chain, which had been staked down into the ground. He picked up the bottle, unscrewed the cap, and began to drink. His surroundings didn't look like the Sahel in Niger. More like forests and savanna, maybe farther south?

"So this guy is a SEAL?" one of the pale faces said.

Lopez turned and frowned.

"He works out of the embassy, definitely one of their special ops guys," said the guy with the accent. Now Lopez placed it as South African. He wore a wide-brimmed hat.

"You're SEAL Team Six, bro?" one of the pale faces asked.

The technically correct answer was to demand to be put in contact with the Red Cross and the U.S. State Department, but Lopez sensed he was past that point. Aside from the South African, the others sounded American.

"Ranger Regiment," he answered.

They all started talking at once.

"What?"

"Like a park ranger?"

"Forest ranger?"

"No," Lopez said. "Army Ranger."

"The Army has Rangers?" one of them asked.

"I thought we were getting a SEAL," another said.

"Are Rangers like SEALs?"

Lopez was about to lose his cool, but he was a captive and had more important things to concern himself with.

"No."

"Are Rangers tougher than SEALs?"

This was starting to sound like a group of grade schoolers. Lopez looked up and examined them one by one. They were all younger guys, probably able-bodied, but Lopez didn't think any of them were particularly impressive physically. Some of them had a dead, vacant look in their eyes that unsettled him, however.

The South African, though. His eyes also told a story. That one looked like a killer.

Lopez got up on his feet and pointed to the manacle clasped around his ankle.

"Why am I here?"

The cluster of young white guys smiled; a few chuckled.

"You haven't told him yet?" one of them asked the South African.

The older man pinched the brim of his hat and nodded. "Be my guest."

One of the nerds stepped forward, trying to suppress a smile and not particularly succeeding.

"You've heard of the big five, I take it?" one of the Americans said.

"No."

"Lion, leopard, elephant, cape buffalo, and rhinoceros. The most desirable hunts among big-game hunters."

"We're burning a lot of daylight here, pal."

"We've each hunted the big five, and now we would like to turn it into the big six. We need a challenge at this point."

The group of young men began opening hard plastic cases and nylon roller bags that they had piled behind them. Bags and cases that Lopez immediately recognized as the type used for transporting weapons.

His blood ran cold as reality settled into place around him.

One by one, they produced a collection of bolt-action rifles, crossbows, and sidearms.

"You see," the American said as he opened the bolt on his rifle and inspected the chamber. "We're hunting the most dangerous game."

He smiled.

"You."

CHAPTER

6

"THAT DOESN'T SOUND very sportsmanlike," Lopez said, regretting how stupid his last words sounded in his mind as he motioned toward the stake pinning him in place.

"Don't be ridiculous," one of the group said. He was a bit on the older side in comparison to the others, maybe forty. "We're giving you a head start."

"You can't be fucking serious," Lopez blurted.

"We thought you might say something like that," one of the hunters said. Several of them walked back to the waiting helicopter and came back with their hands looped under the arms of two manacled men. One of them looked like a local to Lopez, but his clothes were torn, muddy, and blood splotched in a few places.

The other captive was wearing a 5.11 tuxedo.

"Motherfuck," Lopez said under his breath.

"We captured this poacher a few days ago after one of the guys boned his shot and only wounded him," one of the heavyset hunters dragging him along said. "We were going to put him out, but then we came to the conclusion that you might need some added motivation."

"The other one was snatched up in Niamey the same night you were," the South African added. "You two know each other, I take it, since you both worked out of the embassy."

Wallaby and Lopez looked at each other but said nothing. The Army spook shook his head, almost imperceptibly. It was nothing more than a grim acknowledgment of the situation they were in.

The hunters put the alleged poacher on his knees in front of Lopez. The poacher was scowling as he wondered what the hell this was about, screaming in Hausa.

The man on his knees looked up at the hunters and then to Lopez, then back to the hunters with frantic eyes. He spoke in rapid-fire bursts of a local language that the Ranger couldn't understand.

"If you say so, but what's this local guy got to do with me?" Lopez asked, growing increasingly agitated.

"Everything," one of the hunters said, before chambering a round in his rifle.

"What the fuck is this?"

The hunter put the barrel of the rifle to the back of the poacher's head and pulled the trigger. The exit wound sprayed blood and gore onto the ground in front of Lopez before the corpse lurched forward and crashed at his feet. It was an execution. A cold-blooded murder.

Wallaby started shaking. They had him down on his knees as the hunter chambered a fresh round in his rifle.

"Wait!" Lopez exclaimed. "He's more valuable to you alive."

"Yes, we're counting on it," the South African said.

The South African threw the keys to the manacle at Lopez's feet. He then stood to the side of the group and leveled a Browning Hi-Power pistol at his head.

"Half an hour lead time," the South African said. "You run or your friend here has all of his tomorrows canceled indefinitely."

Lopez snatched the key off the ground as one of the hunting party members began the stopwatch function on his watch. Working quickly, he unlocked his manacle and cast it aside. The seven hunters stood poised with their loaded weapons, like a firing squad.

The South African was unwavering, the barrel of his pistol fixed on Lopez. If he put up any resistance at this point, he'd be gunned down immediately. They wanted him to run; they wanted a hunt.

The Ranger began backing away toward the wood line. He took a moment to glance over the faces of each of them, trying to commit the details to memory. Meanwhile, the muscles in his arms and thighs began to shake. It was the adrenaline coursing through his blood, preparing him to run for his life.

"See you soon, Ranger!" one of the hunting party shouted.

But Lopez was already gone, dashing into the forest.

* * *

"See you soon, Ranger!" Henry Williamsburg III shouted at the man's back as he disappeared into the wood line. For the first time in a long time, he felt like himself. Free from prying eyes, expectations, government inquiries, and compliance officers.

The thrill of the chase, the specter of death—all of it brought his life back into focus.

It wasn't totally his fault that he was psychotic. Anyone would be if they had invented what became the world's largest social media website during their freshman year of college. Since then, he had become fabulously wealthy, beyond the imagination of any of the normies. He also hadn't had a single friend since college, being surrounded by corporate sycophants all day.

He looked over the hunting party and knew he was finally with his people. They were his family of choice; they were the new power elite.

It wasn't easy knowing that you'd peaked when you were twenty and everything after that would just be a drag. Just research, execution, and cashing the check. That's why he had to get back to his center. He had finally found a new challenge that excited him.

It had started innocently enough. Once a year he began holding epic events, starting with parties filled with booze, drugs, and the finest hookers flown in from Russia and Eastern Europe. That quickly became tiresome, and he began seeking the next thrill.

That then evolved into wild international travel trips, from scaling Everest to racing rickshaws across the Indian subcontinent. Over time, these trips began to attract like-minded people in the tech space, in Silicon Valley, and they became the go-to event for high-status males. In time these adventure trips became a thing of legend in their community, with the most outrageous rumors flying during water cooler gossip.

A few years back, he'd really gotten into martial arts and firearms. The next thing to do was big-game hunting. His friend, South African–born naturalized US citizen Balthazar Botha, had introduced him to a fellow by the name of Koos DeKlerk. Pushing sixty, DeKlerk was an expert tracker and renowned hunter, not to mention the owner of a shady past connected to South Africa's apartheid regime.

DeKlerk had built a reputation for himself as a safari guide for individuals who wanted to remain discreet. One of his first clients had been a knightly order under the protection of the king of Spain. They were a very conservative Catholic group of elite hunters who wore emblems with their order's motto: *Honoring God by honoring his creatures.*

Just now, DeKlerk was holstering his Browning Hi-Power, but he stood ready with his rifle, watching the tree line.

Henry looked over at Balthazar, observing his drooping face and pale jowls. He didn't look like much but was in fact the wealthiest man in the world, having founded a number of tech companies. Balthazar unfolded the bipod legs on his .300 Win Mag rifle and set it down while he extracted the bolt and applied some gun oil.

Gideon Stephenson stood nearby, counting down the seconds on his smartwatch until they could begin. The smartwatch also monitored Gideon's vital signs, which he tracked religiously, to the point that Henry was surprised he'd been able to break with his anal-retentive routine to go on the hunt.

Gideon was obsessed with immortality and had transformed his home into a kind of laboratory for various antiaging experiments. When you'd invented an algorithm that helped health insurance companies deny patient claims for lifesaving treatments, you had the time and resources for man's oldest quest: unending life.

That algorithm was used extensively by another member of the hunting party, Lance Leisure, who in his late thirties was already the CEO of a major health insurance company. He tooled around as a Manhattan socialite. While Gideon wore outdoor sporting gear, Leisure was dressed for the part in tiger stripe camo fatigues and web gear that he must have bought out of a military surplus catalog.

Another member who had embraced the hunt was Rex Bottoms, who was decked from head to toe in a L.L.Bean starter set straight out of the catalog, safari vest and all. Rex worked in the defense technology investment sector and was well known for his "move fast and break things" attitude.

Then there was Lucas Ramachandran, who had immigrated to the United States as a teenager and quickly became a rising star in Silicon Valley for his "sick" coding. He had founded several companies and made it big, but being a Brahmin was apparently in his blood. He saw their little clique as being part of a new and emerging elite class, a caste really, that would be the catalyst of human evolution through a type of creative destruction. Kali Yuga or whatever.

Wayne Dover worked for a private equity firm and had a background in math but postured himself in public as some sort of quasi scientist and intellectual. He was well known for his many podcast appearances in which he posited various social and scientific theories.

Which brought things full circle to the remaining member of the hunting party.

Gold Copper Silver was one of the intellectual fathers of the ideology they all espoused. Gold had graduated from

Stanford and was deeply involved in the rationalist movement in and around Southern California. However, while experimenting with amphetamines, he had written what became known as a dark enlightenment treatise, which posited that democracy had failed and a new class of übermen must accelerate its collapse to give rise to a new system of governance.

He had continued to develop some of those same themes in later years, writing about archaeofuturism, which explained how liberalism had failed and how humanity's only hope for the future was to return to its agrarian roots and their accompanying hierarchies. Roll back the clock a few hundred years to before the industrial revolution, he said—before the age of enlightenment, even.

Some described him as a neomonarchist, others as a neoreactionary. Whatever the case, he held a PhD in philosophy and was considered something of a rock star within the movement, a comic book villain by those who were not.

Behind them, the plane and helicopter were both spinning up for takeoff. The helicopter would be kept nearby for transportation, but the plane was heading back to an airfield in the capital. The wind from the rotor blades knocked off Gold's cowboy hat. He picked it up, shook the dust off, and stuck it back on his head.

The group shuffled around nervously, looking at their watches, anxious to begin. Together they brandished an assortment of bolt-action tactical and sport rifles for big-game hunting. A couple of the more eccentric members of the crew wielded modernized crossbows and boasted about wanting to get a crossbow kill.

Henry looked down at his watch.

It wasn't the first time they had hunted man. DeKlerk had taken them out on safari before, to national parks across Africa where they hunted poachers for sport. A good deal for the South African, as he got paid twice: once for protecting the rhinos and elephants in the park, a second time by the hunters helping with that protection.

But this was the first time they had hunted a professional, a genuine contender. He was a special operations soldier, one of America's best. He was a real challenge. A predator, like they were. Henry had always kind of seen himself as being the Navy SEAL of the business world.

The social media tech mogul looked back to his watch—well, actually it was the Ranger's Par Weber watch—as it counted down the minutes.

May the best man win.

CHAPTER 7

LOPEZ RAN.

The forest trees whizzed by as his legs carried him faster than he could ever recall running before. Hunted, he felt like an animal. The Ranger dodged around bushes and vaulted over streams. After nearly twenty minutes at a dead sprint, he slowed down, knowing that he needed to put some initial distance between himself and his pursuers but that in order to survive, deception would be more important than distance.

He knew he had left signs of his passage behind him, spoor such as footprints, bent grass, and broken tree limbs, which would lead even a semicompetent tracker straight toward him sure as a freight train barreling down railroad tracks.

As he slowed to a jog, his heart threatened to beat out of his chest. His beating heart warned him of his own mortality. He clenched his eyes shut for a moment as an old familiar feeling washed over him. It was something he had felt in combat in Afghanistan as a younger man, something he had felt just days ago in Niger.

I will never feel as alive as I feel at this moment.

His eyes darted across the forest floor, searching. Unlike the way it appeared in the movies, fashioning a bow and arrows with raw material found in the wilderness was an exhausting and time-consuming process. Time and energy were very much finite resources in Lopez's situation. Even sharpening a rock and tying it to a stick to create a spear took up a lot more time and effort than most people suspected, which was one of the lessons he'd learned in SERE school on Fort Bragg.

Pushing aside some dried brush, he did find a small tree branch that had fallen long before because it was bleached, the bark long gone. At the end of it was a knot in the wood, perfect for striking. A simple club was the best improvised weapon he could hope for in the near term, and now he had one.

While he momentarily paused to pick up the club, he also forced himself to do something else he'd learned in the military. It was called *stop, look, listen, smell*, or SLLS, because the Army loved acronyms. What it meant was that while on patrol, a Ranger should occasionally make a security halt and use his senses, pushing them deeper into the forest, in order to search for signs of the enemy.

He smelled the dry desert dust mixed with some rot and decay emanating from the forest growth. He was where the Sahel turned to forest before turning to jungle. What he saw was knee-high brown-and-green savanna grass in all directions, with scattered brush and trees that turned the area green. Some areas looked rocky, others were wide-open clearings, and some parts of the region appeared to be thickly vegetated.

He heard before he saw a herd of elephants moving laterally to him maybe a hundred meters ahead. He counted what looked like four adults and three juveniles in the herd. The large gray shapes lumbered forward slowly through the brush, unconcerned for the moment about what was going on nearby.

The hunters had far more resources, not to mention weapons, than he. However, Lopez had a couple of things in his favor. Raw strength and physical endurance were two of them. The other was tactical patience. He understood how to use the terrain to his advantage, and when to strike the enemy at a time of his choosing.

After putting some distance between himself and the hunters before they began pursuing, his next thought was to do the opposite of what they expected of their prey.

The game was on, and it wasn't just his life that was on the line.

How in the goddamn hell did Wallaby get captured?

Then he reluctantly conceded to himself that Wallaby had probably gotten caught the same way he had.

Cassandra.

CHAPTER

8

GIDEON AND LUCAS crept through the forest brush. The South African had picked up the spoor for them and pointed them in the right direction. From there, it was relatively easy for the duo to follow a big dumb Ranger stomping through the woods on their own. Many of the footprints in the soft red sand, especially around the banks of streams, were easy to detect.

"I'm already doing the plasma transfusions," Lucas said, trying to impress while pretending to be nonchalant.

"You should look into stem cell therapies next," Gideon replied. "There's a clinic in Próspera I can refer you to if you like."

Gideon was one of the world's foremost experts on the quest for immortality, having used his immense fortune to perform endless medical experiments on himself. His birth certificate said he was forty-one years old, but he could easily be mistaken for a man ten years younger, as long as one didn't look too closely. A far cry from immortality but a work in progress nonetheless.

Lucas, like the other self-proclaimed high-status males in their group, wanted to defeat not just the cultural norms, laws, regulations, and taxes that they felt constrained by but also existence itself by blasting off into the stars and living forever.

The two hunters proceeded forward, approaching a waterfall up ahead. They heard the crashing water before they saw it.

"What did you say that protocol was called again?" Lucas asked. He was known to be a sick coder, but biotech wasn't really his field.

"The Organ Blueprint," Gideon replied. "A doctor designed it to literally measure what each of your organs needs and then treat them with that protocol in order to reverse the aging process."

"Can you help me sync up with that doctor?" Lucas could scarcely contain his admiration. While he himself was known as a "unicorn" in the venture capital world, Gideon was a decaunicorn. In other words, Gideon was worth over ten billion dollars while Lucas was worth merely a billion. Anyone could be a billionaire these days, and in the venture capital world it didn't mean much at this point.

"But of course," Gideon said, his pasty-white skin stretching across his skull as he took on a facial expression reminiscent of a smile.

Up ahead, their path narrowed onto a stone cliff. The rock made a staircase shape with a drop-off at the top, from which a small waterfall gushed downward before breaking on the rockwork below, leveling out for about five feet, and continuing off the next drop about fifteen feet down into a pond. Down below, a few dozen gazelles occupied the watering hole, hanging out in the shade near the edge of the pond.

The footprints, of course, were obliterated on the slick rock around the waterfall, but the cardinal direction was clear enough. They would pick up the spoor on the other side.

As they skirted around the waterfall, Lucas couldn't help himself. He had always wanted to meet Gideon, and getting invited on the hunting expedition along with his idols was a dream come true.

"So what's the difference between a SEAL and a Ranger?" Lucas asked.

"Um, I'm not sure," Gideon replied. "SEALs are tougher than Rangers, right?"

With Lucas in the lead, they carefully moved across the cliff edge, trying to step over the water but still getting wet up to their ankles.

"I thought Marines were the toughest."

"Maybe that's right. It's Marines, then SEALs, then Rangers."

"So this guy is just a Ranger?" Lucas said dejectedly. "Maybe next time DeKlerk can get a Marine."

Gideon chuckled and was beginning to say something when a massive rock slammed down from above right onto Lucas's head, cracking his neck into an unnatural right angle with an audible crunch before his grip on his rifle failed and his body pitched sideways and fell into the pond, scattering the gazelles in every direction.

Lucas landed with a splash and sank to the bottom of the pond.

CHAPTER

9

LOPEZ HELD THE rock high above his head with both hands as he loomed over the two hunters.

He'd buttonhooked backward to ambush his own spoor about half an hour prior, knowing that some of the hunters would be hot on his trail. It was a classic tactic, and these two hunters appeared to be undisciplined as they talked and made noises while stalking him. They must have thought he was much farther away.

"So this guy is just a Ranger?" Lopez heard the younger one ask even over the sound of the waterfall. "Maybe next time DeKlerk can get a Marine."

Lopez noted the name DeKlerk just as he launched the rock over the side of the cliff at the lead hunter. It was with no small amount of satisfaction that he heard the hunter's neck snap like a twig before he pitched over the side of the cliff and scattered the local wildlife.

But the other hunter reacted far faster than Lopez had anticipated. Without missing a beat, the second hunter, who was whiter than Casper, pivoted on the balls of his feet and brought his crossbow up to his shoulder. Lopez dove to the side as an arrow tipped with razor-sharp prongs passed less than a foot from his head and sailed into the forest behind him.

Lopez was hard, not stupid. He wasn't about to take on the crossbow-carrying albino with only the club tucked into his pants. Staying low, he scrambled on all fours away from the edge of the cliff and then took off running back into the forest.

He knew he was going to have to be smart if he wanted to survive, but it wasn't just a question of outwitting his opponents, even with superior tactics. Mostly, he just had to avoid making a lot of small but deadly mistakes. For instance, sticking around trying to fight a guy armed with a crossbow would be a deadly mistake. If he could manage that, then he could nickel-and-dime the hunting party one by one until they were reduced to the point that he could take them on directly.

Running toward a trio of trees, he took cover and watched to see if he was being followed. Seconds seemed to pass like hours, but there was no sign of the albino. Maybe the death of his late comrade had frayed his nerves, and if so, that was a good sign. These guys could be taken apart and broken, both physically and psychologically.

The hunting party was down from nine to eight, and he had a name.

DeKlerk.

Sounded South African.

Maybe next time DeKlerk *could* get a Marine, the same way DeKlerk and Cassandra had gotten a Ranger this time, he thought to himself.

Lopez looked forward to getting his hands around both of their throats.

CHAPTER

10

HENRY LISTENED INTO the handheld shortwave radio from the party's security halt in the forest a few kilometers away. Gideon was talking a mile a minute. He was scared, and upset, but there was something else in his voice too. Henry recognized it as excitement.

"Dead? Are you sure?" Henry asked.

Gideon's breathless narration crackled over the radio as DeKlerk attempted to listen in as he stepped toward Henry.

"Which one is dead?" DeKlerk asked.

"Lucas," Henry answered.

"Is that the colored one?"

"Uh, yeah, I think his family is from India."

"No matter, then."

Off to the side, Balthazar feigned an aghast look at his fellow South African's crass racism. It wasn't that Balthazar, also a child of apartheid, wasn't racist. It was just that he considered himself to be pan-Aryan, which was why he'd permitted Lucas on their hunting trip, as he was ethnically Indo-Aryan and therefore a part of the master race.

That said, he moved on with a shrug and bit into a Clif Bar, chewing with his mouth open.

The other hunters didn't seem particularly bothered either. They had been out in groups of two, scouting forward searching for Lopez, but DeKlerk had gotten Gideon and Lucas fixed on the spoor, and so they took the lead. Now they were reconsolidating in one location, with Gideon rambling almost incoherently over the radio as he ran back toward them.

They'd never actually had one of their members killed, and this was a new experience for the hunting party personally and for DeKlerk professionally. Seriously injured people, sure, but not dead. DeKlerk had never lost a client on safari. He'd once had one bitten in the ass by a lion, and on multiple occasions he'd had to evacuate people who came down with dysentery while they were out in the field, but that was the extent of it.

But the hunting party had to keep pushing the limits. A hundred Thai hookers weren't even enough to satisfy them; no, they wanted the next challenge. Killing poachers had been a fun diversion. For a group of people who loved to flaunt society's rules, norms, and laws, breaking the ultimate taboo, specifically murder, was one they relished.

DeKlerk looked up into the sky as Gideon came stumbling back into their ad hoc camp. He was white as a sheet, but that was his normal complexion. He kept rattling off the details of Lucas's death, discussing how the rock had crushed his head, how he'd fallen into the water, and how he, Gideon, had fired off an arrow at the Ranger before he got away.

The immortality guru was fascinated by death and killing, even if it was one of his comrades who ate it.

But it was already late afternoon, the South African noted. You could run a combat tracking patrol at night if you really knew what you were doing and were working with trained, disciplined professionals. However, these were not trained, disciplined professionals. They would have to regroup and take another crack at Lopez in the morning.

They'd box him in from multiple sides, then move in for the kill once he had nowhere to go. Simple tactics were often the most effective. Until then, he knew he wouldn't sleep well. They would have to maintain a guard on their camp as a precaution against the unlikely event that the Ranger doubled back and tried to ambush them in the night.

DeKlerk drank from his canteen before screwing the cap back on and sliding it into a pouch on his belt. Standing up from the rock he was sitting on, he headed over to begin briefing his clients. "Come on, boys," he encouraged them. "We'll wrap everything up tomorrow morning."

CHAPTER

11

THE RAIN CAME down in sheets, and Lopez was especially grateful for two reasons.

The first was that he had not had time to attempt some countertracking techniques to try to erase his footprints, but with the rain obliterating his spoor, he didn't have to worry about that. The second was that he was dehydrated as hell from evading through the forest all day.

He doglegged into what he suspected would be a good lie-up site for the night. Sure enough, he found a hollow in a tree that would offer at least some minimal shelter from the rain. Considering he was being hunted like a dog by a pack of rifle- and crossbow-toting psychopaths, he was surprisingly comfortable.

Rangers were night fighters. The hunters were not going to be stalking him through the rain at night, especially if they didn't have night vision devices. The safari guide, DeKlerk would, but not the hunting party of softer Americans.

Already soaking wet, Lopez took off his T-shirt and found some low-hanging tree branches. It took a few minutes, but he was able to tie the two sleeves and the bottom corners of the shirt to the thinnest parts where the branches became twigs. Stretched out like that and facing the sky, the T-shirt became an improvised rain catcher.

Next, he went searching for a small rock, which he placed in the center of the shirt. He cursed as one of his tie-downs sprang loose and he had to start over again. He got the rain catcher tied up and tried with the rock again, and this time it held.

The rock created a low point in the center of the catcher, from which the rainwater absorbed by the T-shirt would drip down. Lopez was relieved when he saw a slow but steady drip of water coming from the bottom of his rain catcher. He had found a capless plastic bottle during the day (humans dumped their trash everywhere, even in the remote African plains), and now he placed it underneath the rain catcher to collect the water.

In a survival situation, the priorities were water, food, and shelter. Without water, his muscles would start to seize up and he would eventually suffer heat exhaustion. A person could survive for three days without water, but the key word was *survive*. Lying under a tree waiting to be rescued was one thing. Escaping and evading through the forest placed additional burdens on the body. Once his resources were depleted, the hunting party would be able to run down and kill their prey. His goal was to make sure that didn't happen.

The minimal protection provided by the tree he found would have to do for shelter. He didn't think he would have much luck stomping around at night trying to find the materials to make a lean-to. As far as food, he would have to work on that tomorrow.

There were a lot of myths out there about outdoorsmen and survivalists. Foraging for food in the wilderness was in itself an exhausting, full-time job. If you were living off the land like that, there was little chance that you were also doing something else, much less something like military patrol. He would have to graze off the land as he could, but Lopez knew there was no way he would be able to stop long enough to fashion weapons and hunt wildlife.

He drank greedily from the plastic container before it was halfway full, then set it back in position to collect more water.

Crawling into the hollow in the tree protected him from most of the incoming rain, but shirtless and soaking wet, he was starting to shiver. He hugged himself to try to retain some warmth. Listening to the raindrops descending through the trees, he rested his head against the tree and stared out into the night.

That was when it happened; that was always when it happened. When things slowed down, the brain was able to begin processing what it had experienced. The terror of what he was experiencing was beginning to set in. He was being hunted for sport like a wild animal. The odds of his survival were slim to none; that was just the reality. It didn't matter what a badass he was. The fact was that they had guns and he didn't.

The terror was instinctual, natural, and primeval. But then his training and conditioning took over. He was a

Ranger; he was trained to defy the odds and subvert the enemy's expectations. He had participated in bloody combat from Afghanistan to West Africa. Lopez wasn't anyone's victim, today or ever.

It was at times like this, quiet moments of reflection and doubt, that a man needed something to fall back on. For some it was their religious faith, believing in a higher power. For Lopez, it was the Ranger Creed that every Ranger lived by.

Based on the conversations of the hunters he had overheard, they didn't even really know anything about the Ranger Regiment, which wasn't surprising. Even many pro-military Americans would look at you weird if you mentioned you were an Army Ranger. Their frame of reference was park rangers at a national park.

The history of the Rangers went all the way back to the 1600s and colonial America. However, the modern Ranger battalions had first arisen in 1974. In the aftermath of the Vietnam War, when the postwar Army was riddled with drugs and disciplinary issues, the Rangers had been set up to serve as a standard bearer, an example of what an elite soldier could be during troubled times.

Within that small and often misunderstood unit was a single even-more-secretive company of about forty Rangers: his outfit, the Regimental Reconnaissance Company. An elite within the elite.

The Ranger Creed itself had been penned back in the seventies by the unit's first command sergeant major. Six stanzas, each providing guidance in the absence of direct orders. The creed stated plainly that surrender was not a

Ranger word. In the absence of orders, those were his orders: fight, survive, do not quit. Surrender was not a Ranger word. *Never shall I leave a fallen comrade.*

That meant Wallaby, who was being held by these creeps.

When the hunting party had confronted him earlier in the day, he had made an effort to memorize as many details of their faces as possible. There were two of them that he had a vague recollection of, but it was hard to place them. He had never met them in person, he was sure of that, but he could have sworn he'd seen them on television before. Had they been giving a press conference? Offering testimony in front of Congress?

Something like that. His recollection felt foggy, even if the answer was on the tip of his tongue.

They must be somebody back in the world. Only wealthy people went on safari to hunt big game for their trophy wall. What kind of people paid to hunt human beings? The überwealthy. The Masters of the Universe. Illuminati-type shit.

As he began to drift off to sleep, he thought for a moment about his father, who he had never met, and about his grandfather, who he hadn't spoken to in years. He had been raised by his grandpa, whose own service as a Marine in the Vietnam War had forever scarred him. He'd forbidden his grandson from joining the military.

But Lopez had been a young man, often in trouble in his hometown in rural Alabama, and there happened to be a war on in Afghanistan and then in Syria. He needed to get out of Dodge, and college wasn't a realistic possibility.

His grandpa hadn't spoken to him since the day he enlisted. When he went home on leave, he would stay with an aunt or a family friend. His grandpa didn't want anything to do with him.

Then his chin sagged into his chest, the lights switched off, and he slept.

CHAPTER

12

BALTHAZAR GRIMACED AS he looked upward toward the tarp that DeKlerk had strung up to protect them from the rain in their makeshift camp. Normally, he and Henry were both surrounded by a small army of bodyguards and personal assistants, but out here they had to maintain as small a footprint as possible to keep their manhunts shrouded in secrecy.

Tonight, DeKlerk was standing guard himself while the others relaxed.

Gold, who was conversing with Dover, was clearly more comfortable with the natural world than the other man was.

"I think about the extinction of megafauna every day," Gold lamented.

"You mean like the woolly mammoth?" Dover asked.

"The mammoth, giant sloths, giant armadillos, all of them. I feel their loss weighing me down emotionally every day."

"I can probably clone new ones," Balthazar interjected.

"I think you should," Gold said. The others hung on his words; he was, after all, the founder of the dark enlightenment movement. "In fact, the restoration of megafauna should be a key pillar of archaeofuturism, creating a future that looks more like our agrarian past. Now is the time, as so many are waking up to the failures of liberalism and democracy."

"To bring about the ethnostate?" Dover asked. "Like the Chinese are doing?"

"It's the only way." Gideon spoke up. "The degenerate races are simply never going to be productive enough to meet the world's needs."

Gold nodded. His students having learned his lessons well, he let them continue.

"The enlightenment led to modernity, which led to the twin failures of liberalism and democracy," Balthazar said, perhaps reciting from some obscure book. Maybe one of Gold's books.

"So the goal is to turn back the clock while also looking to the future," Gideon said. "Revert to our agrarian and monarchist roots using those first principles, not those of the humanists that created this convergence of crisis called the modern world."

"Correct," Gold said. "However, archaeofuturism isn't about nostalgia for the past; rather, we simply look to the past for a workable model of social hierarchy—you know, like a labor class, a warrior caste, a monarchy of high-status males, and so on."

Dover, being a pretend intellectual, now found himself touching a live wire. They were all fellow travelers, but he would never have been so forthright. Then again, they were in a camp in the middle of the African forest. No one need ever know.

"It does seem that the ethnostate is the only solution to the stalled engine of democracy. Even the left calls it late-stage capitalism. Everyone knows it's a failure."

"That's why it falls upon Henry and Balthazar to use their social media empires to indoctrinate the youth."

Henry, who had listened quietly thus far, smiled. "Memetic warfare," he said.

Lance, the health insurance company CEO, looked a bit lost.

"You have a role to play as well," Gold said, sensing his opportunity to get his hooks into Lance. "Managing health insurance companies, you can steer much of the medical science, helping your friends artificially extend their lifespans and denying health care to the degenerate races and paupers."

"My company is already pretty good at denying health insurance claims, but what does memetic warfare entail?" Lance asked.

"Think of it as applied sociology," Henry said.

"Cultural engineering," Balthazar added.

"Basically, it's just advertising and game theory in its most basic form," Henry said. "We use our social media companies to advance ideas—small, innocuous ones even—that are intended to eventually rewire culture by rewiring human brains. Hey, we're just asking questions here, after all. Some people call it micro-influencing. People don't even realize they're receiving propaganda."

"We use easily remembered imagery, triggering events, to prepare the populace for what comes next." Balthazar shrugged. "It's not even that hard once you know which buttons to press. Grievance politics, illegal aliens, black violence, the Jews. It's just basic stuff that people already believe in but have suppressed due to how liberalism has socialized them over the last fifty years."

"All right, advertising makes sense," Lance said. "But what is the product you're selling? I get that it's the dark enlightenment, but what do you want people to do with that information?"

Balthazar smiled. "We're not revisionists; we want a revolution so that something new can be born from the creative destruction."

"To what end?"

"To install a new regime and create a new type of human species."

CHAPTER

13

Lopez woke up to the familiar thump of helicopter rotor blades. He had slept fitfully through the night, but it was better than nothing. He tore down his T-shirt, squeezed as much water out of it into the container as possible, and put it back on, all the while listening to the sounds of the helicopter to try to figure out where it was going.

It sounded as though it was coming from the direction he had traveled and heading in the same direction he was, so moving from roughly north to south based on the position of the sun.

Then it dawned on him, and Lopez knew what they were doing.

They had called the helicopter in to shuttle some of the hunters to blocking positions up ahead of him. Classic hammer-and-anvil strategy. Other hunters would flush him toward the blocking positions, and he would be penned in with nowhere to run. It was pretty typical combat tracking tactics he knew from his Army training.

There were eight members of the hunting party, so that meant they would be in two groups of four or four groups of two. The Ranger knew he could outpace the dough-faced hunting party, but he wasn't going to be able to outrun a helicopter.

He chugged the rest of the water that had collected in the container, retrieved his club, and started moving out, heading west, so as to escape the hunters he was certain had deployed to the north and south. They wouldn't have any spoor to follow after the previous night's rainfall, so they would probably spread out and sweep him toward the blocking positions.

For good measure, he broke off a tree branch and used it to sweep away his footprints as he left the site. It wouldn't fool a good tracker, but there were damn few good trackers out there.

Lopez quickened his pace as he heard voices somewhere behind him. He had already established that the hunters had poor noise discipline, but they were closer than he expected.

Somehow, he knew that this was the day that would make him or break him.

* * *

The middle-aged South African hunter knelt and took off his hat, which he used to fan himself.

"This was his bed-down site," he announced. "Spoor leads off in that direction," he said, pointing west. "He tried to sweep over his footprints when he left this morning, but you can tell from the high sign what direction he went in."

"High sign?" Balthazar asked.

"Look at the branches pushed aside; look at how the grass is bent right over there," he said, pointing.

"I don't see it," the tech mogul muttered, readjusting his floppy-brimmed camo hat.

"It takes time to train the eye to see these things. We'll split up into two teams and move out in the same direction as our game, with about a two-hundred-meter separation between us. Balthazar with me. Wayne and Lance, you're paired up on the other side of us."

The hunters nodded and readied their weapons. Rex, Gold, Gideon, and Henry were manning the blocking positions where the helicopter had dropped them off about thirty minutes ago.

DeKlerk put his hat back in place and stood. He had learned his trade well decades prior in a South African paramilitary unit in South West Africa. Tracking was both a science and an art, one that took years to develop.

The essence of tactical tracking was following spoor, or signs left behind by the passage of man. These could be tracks or footprints as well as the high signs he had mentioned. Footprints were the low signs, which could also include other tells, such as flattened earth that had been walked on, snapped sticks that had been stepped on, or leaves on the forest floor that had been disturbed by the dragging of feet.

The high signs were other tells of passage up off the forest floor. These included brush that had been bent as the quarry passed, branches that had been moved out of the way or broken, or bark skinned off a tree as someone brushed against it. Other, even more obvious signs he would look for included litter left behind by their prey, pieces of clothing torn and hung up on thornbushes, or even a blood trail if the man was injured.

His skills had been developed in Kenya during the Rhodesian Bush War, and he had also plied them in South Africa's bloody little "border war" in the 1980s.

DeKlerk motioned to the hunters.

"Let's get after it, then."

* * *

Lopez ran, again attempting to distance himself from the hunters to give himself room to breathe, time to maneuver. They were already on his tracks, so for the time being he didn't worry about them seeing the fresh ones as his feet sank into the soft earth.

Coming to a hill, he scrambled up, using tree branches and exposed roots as handholds. The trees offered good cover and concealment from the ground, but if the hunters had the helicopter up looking for him, then there was really nowhere he could hide.

On the top of the hill, he came to a small clearing and began to employ some countertracking techniques. Distance wasn't going to save him; they had a helicopter, for Christ's sake. Deception was key.

Walking through the clearing, he made sure he left some very clear tracks, then leapt away onto some rocks at a right angle, away from his own trail. The Ranger then stepped on the rocks and onto some hard-packed dirt to avoid leaving signs of his abrupt change in direction.

Lopez was no expert tracker or countertracker, but the Army had sent him to a tactical tracking course in Arizona several years ago. The skills he had learned there had aided him on missions in Afghanistan and on the African continent. A sharp change in direction was known as the most surefire way to throw off a tracking team.

He repeated this maneuver a couple more times, every few hundred meters, making an abrupt change in direction to hopefully throw the hunters off his trail.

CHAPTER

14

"YOU SEE THAT?" DeKlerk pointed. "He made an abrupt change in direction to try to throw us off his spoor. Classic countertracking technique."

"Where did you learn so much about all this stuff?" Lance asked.

"Many years ago, in a war no one remembers. South Africa had a so-called border war decades ago. I spent a lot of time in South West Africa, now called Namibia."

After walking side by side, following Lopez's trail for about an hour, the two teams had once again converged on his spoor as DeKlerk worked to ascertain his new direction of travel. Amateurs in the tracking game followed the trail at their feet, literally looking straight down and trying to follow the prints.

Experienced trackers followed spoor that was thirty to forty feet in front of them, which offered better depth perception and was faster than looking for each individual footprint. By using this technique, DeKlerk's experienced eyes were able to quickly detect the attempted deception.

"I figured you were an old South African Defence Force hand," Balthazar said. "You got that smell on you."

DeKlerk shook his head.

"Not SADF, not military. Police paramilitary unit. It was called Koevoet, or Crowbar in English. We did lots of tracking ops. Killed loads of munts in the 1980s."

"How was—" Lance began to ask.

"Now then," DeKlerk interrupted, not interested in speaking any further about his past. "Get on thataway," he said, pointing in the Ranger's new direction of travel.

* * *

Lopez struggled through the brush, noticing that it was getting greener and thicker as he traveled, as if the terrain was transitioning from one biome to another. The thing was, he still had no idea where he was. It didn't look much like Niger, but based on the terrain and vegetation, his best assessment was that he was still in West Africa.

Behind him a flock of birds burst from the trees and soared into the blue sky. They had been disturbed on the hilltop that he had just traversed. He was still being tracked. That wasn't good. One of them, almost certainly DeKlerk, was a professional tracker.

While moving through waist-high palm fronds, he made another attempt at countertracking. This time he stopped, looked over his shoulder, and carefully walked backward, making sure to step inside the footprints he had just left behind. Then, after laying a false trail for his pursuers, he moved out in another direction.

With a little luck, they would take the bait and continue in his original direction of movement.

He was heading south again, moving over relatively flat terrain. He gripped his improvised club in his right hand, acutely aware of how naked he felt out here alone, unarmed, without any of his usual go-to-war gear.

With the foliage thickening, he had another idea. The Ranger began to circle back around to ambush his own spoor. From a concealed position, he would be able to see if the hunting party was still on his trail and gather some intel on them at the same time.

He wiped sweat from his forehead. The sun was growing high in the sky but felt like it was hovering right over his head.

Taking his time to carefully buttonhook back around on his own spoor, he found a position that offered some concealment as well as a view of the area he had made passage through just minutes prior.

He was now in a wetter area from which the previous night's rainfall had not yet drained or evaporated. Reaching down into the mud at his feet, he used it to coat his face and bare forearms.

The improvised camouflage would prevent his skin's reflective surface from compromising his position. That was why soldiers used camouflage paint in the field—not because their white skin didn't blend in but rather because human skin across the board reflected light. That's right; even the brothers needed to camo up on patrol, as per Ranger standard operating procedures.

To his astonishment, he hadn't even finished smearing the mud on himself when he heard muted voices nearby.

* * *

"You know, there is a certain geometry to venture capitalism. Why make ten million dollars when you can just make thirty-five million dollars instead?"

Balthazar blinked and suddenly turned around to face Lance.

"I'm sorry, did you say something?"

"Uh, nah, nothing," Lance replied dejectedly.

Balthazar lived in his own world.

Wayne was up front with DeKlerk, the South African safari guide, who was again taking a knee and examining something that none of the others in the group could see. To them, tracking and fieldcraft were a type of black magic, maybe one of the few they had never really learned.

After all, if black magic was the use of signs and symbolism to bring new realities into existence, perhaps tracking wasn't entirely different.

"Look there," DeKlerk said, falling into instructor mode.

When he looked carefully, Wayne could make out the light imprint of booted footprints.

"Oh, there they are!" Wayne blurted. "Wow, I saw them. You know, I could be a really good tracker. I know I would be one of the best. I'm largely a self-taught guy."

DeKlerk's ice-blue eyes drilled holes through the man. If Wayne weren't paying him, he thought, he might drill through his skull with a rifle shot, or an electric drill, or maybe just a sharp stick through the eye socket.

"You missed it," DeKlerk announced, taking the wind out of his sails.

"Missed what?" Wayne said. "I don't miss things."

"Almost everyone steps from heel to toe, so there is a deep depression in the soil around the heel. This has been true of this Ranger all day, but now, look, suddenly the footprints change. The deeper depression is at the toes. The impact points are reversed. What does that tell us?"

Wayne's eyes looked panicked, as if he had been given a math problem he couldn't solve.

"It means he started walking backwards," Balthazar said as he walked up behind them, pursing his lips after he'd bested Wayne.

"Correct," DeKlerk said. "But moreover, he walked backwards on his own tracks. See how these tracks just disappear up ahead? He changed directions again."

The South African looked left, then right, then left again and began walking into the grass.

DeKlerk circled around in the tall grass for several minutes before announcing, "Here are the new prints. He's heading south."

DeKlerk slung his rifle and reached for a small handheld radio clipped to his belt. Turning it on, he moved the dial to the correct channel and spoke into it.

"BP One and BP Two, this is Safari One. I want both of you to displace five hundred meters to the west of your current location for a better intercept location."

Blocking positions one and two both acknowledged the instructions.

"We've got him now," DeKlerk announced. "There's just a few kilometers between us and the blocking positions, with the Ranger running straight into them and us right behind."

Balthazar nodded and took the lead, the muzzle of his rifle pointing the way.

CHAPTER

15

LOPEZ HEARD THE muted voices before he saw them, a party of four following right along and paralleling the footprints he had left in the dirt before circling around back on them himself.

The fatter guy in the lead was one of the hunters he vaguely recalled seeing on television sometime in the past. He had a bolt-action rifle, large caliber if Lopez's suspicion was correct, and was stalking forward carefully, in anticipation of contact.

Behind him was the South African safari guide, and trailing not far behind were two more hunters. One carried a crossbow and the other a rifle. Lopez recalled that, when he'd seen the whole party at close range, most of them appeared to be carrying high-end Sako 90 bolt guns with what looked like Swarovski hunting scopes. A few of the hunters had carried a different rifle, though, perhaps a Bergara B-14 Wilderness HMR.

The four-man hunting party was creeping forward, and in a few hundred meters would begin to see that he had changed direction yet again. The old South African would then realize what had happened and that they were under observation. Lopez had to make a decision.

It wasn't an easy one to make. Each inflection point was a flash in time, each of which could easily end his life. Instincts took over. Fill the void with pure aggression.

Breaking cover, Lopez stayed low and moved slowly, stepping from heel to toe across the forest floor. The stories about woodsmen who were completely silent while moving through the wilderness were a total myth, but it was possible to use some techniques to remain as stealthy as possible as long as possible. Taking careful steps to minimize sound helped, as did staying low to avoid silhouetting yourself against the horizon.

The proper use of cover, concealment, and camouflage were all critical, but realistically, it was the damp ground that helped him remain quiet as he moved more than any particular skill he applied.

He focused on the two in the rear, who had let a separation of thirty meters or so grow between them and the two up front. He saw the clothing of the two flash between individual blades of grass as he silently crept up on them.

His heart threatened to beat out of his chest as sweat streamed down his face.

He felt like a wolf, his senses heightened and alert for anything. Adrenaline coursed through his bloodstream in anticipation. Suddenly, everything seemed possible.

Now he was behind them, and they had no idea. He was close enough to hear their voices, close enough to smell them. He had achieved tactical surprise.

"I discovered a new law of physics, but the quacks in academia didn't understand it," the one with the crossbow was saying to his partner. "It's like, I don't have time to explain fourteen-dimensional space, the omniverse, and the theory of everything to a bunch of hostile scientists and professional navel gazers who are trying to take me down."

Lopez heard the words, but his brain didn't process them. He didn't care; they were irrelevant to his objective, which was to kill.

He gripped the wooden club in his gnarled fist until his knuckles turned white.

"They were just a bunch of gatekeepers," his target was saying. "They don't understand how the f-force wave affects quantum mechanics."

"Yeah, quantum is a big thing," the guy in front of him replied.

Lopez came right up behind the crossbow-wielding pseudo-intellectual scientist. Now he was at arm's length distance and had a full view of the man's pear-shaped physique and lunch lady haircut.

He didn't hesitate.

The Ranger's arm swung back over his shoulder, and then his shoulder socket acted like a lever that swung the club down on the back of the man's head with maximum force. The knotted end of the broken tree limb made a crunching sound as it hit the back of his skull.

The fat man went limp, folded like an empty trench coat, and collapsed to the forest floor.

Lopez swung the club three more times, hitting the sweaty man in the temple, then missing and striking into the dirt, and then catching him one more time in the back of the skull. The fat man's eyes stared straight ahead, wide open but unmoving. It all transpired in a matter of a few seconds.

"Wayne?" the rifle-carrying hunter asked, having heard something. He turned and almost jumped out of his own skin at the sight of a mud-covered Ranger flipping over his friend's lifeless body. He looked like a creature that had literally emerged from the swamp.

His eyes moved downward, seeing the swamp creature reaching for Wayne's crossbow.

Adrenaline surged through Lance's entire body, his heart rate shooting up to something close to 120 beats per minute. Although he made decisions at his health insurance company that killed people deader than a doornail every single day, he had very little personal relationship with death and none with directly killing something that could kill him.

Fine motor control was the first thing to go as Lance fumble fucked with the bolt on his rifle. The crossbow was making its way into the swamp creature's hands, but Lance had started with his rifle at the ready, and even caught by surprise, he brought it into action first.

He squeezed the trigger, but nothing happened, then squeezed it again with the same result.

The swamp creature was suddenly on a knee, the crossbow having fully materialized in his hands.

Lance was staring right at the pointy end of an arrow as it launched toward him.

CHAPTER

16

THE ARROW FLEW a distance of no more than seven meters, glancing off Lance's rifle and slicing a deep furrow through his shoulder on its way to disappearing into the forest somewhere behind him. The wound immediately began to bleed, and he could feel the warmth of his own blood escaping his body and dripping down his arm, turning his shirt sleeve red.

The swamp man turned and ran, vanishing into the forest amid a crash of vegetation.

Then Lance felt like his eardrums exploded.

Balthazar worked the bolt on his .300 Win Mag rifle and fired again, then again, trying to suss out their prey. Then DeKlerk was standing next to him as well, shouting something into his radio.

He turned to say something to Lance.

"What?"

"Your safety! Flick the bloody safety off!"

Lance looked down and sheepishly thumbed down the safety catch on his rifle, which would allow the weapon to fire.

Then Balthazar was shooting again, his bullets echoing through the forest.

* * *

Lopez ran.

He ran until his legs felt like they were filled with battery acid and his lungs refused to gulp down the oxygen he needed. Then he pushed himself harder.

Gunshots sounded behind him, the shots passing just to his left and slamming into a tree to his front, showering him with splinters as he ran. He slid down an embankment and kept going, even as more gunfire sounded.

He used the sling attached to the crossbow to throw it over his back. He noted several arrows in the quiver mounted to the underside of it, but he didn't dare pause and figure out how to reload the weapon. He had never fired a crossbow before just now. It really wasn't a weapon with a military application in this day and age.

He busted through thicker bush, making his way forward, but then realized his back was exposed to the embankment he had just slid down. Glancing over his shoulder, he saw three figures suddenly burst to the edge of the embankment.

Lopez cut a zigzag pattern, changing directions drastically as he ran away. Bullets were tearing up the foliage all around him, but his constant movement made it hard for the hunters to lock onto their target.

A rifle round kicked up dirt at his feet as the Ranger lunged toward the tree line. He slipped on the underbrush and rolled across a rock as he heard shouts and more gunfire. Then, suddenly, he was airborne, falling off a cliff he hadn't known was there.

Time seemed to stand still for one dreadful moment.

Then the ground came up to meet him.

* * *

DeKlerk led the two hunters forward as his radio chirped in his hand. He was speaking to the four others on the blocking positions, making sure they were on track to intercept the Ranger on his current trajectory.

"He's just a few hundred meters ahead," DeKlerk announced. "Finish him off."

Lance looked frightened and turned to Balthazar.

"Do you think Wayne is going to make it?"

Balthazar's lips made an upside-down U shape for a moment. "Nope."

"You're sure? I didn't check on him before we left."

"He was still breathing, but he would never have made it," the social media and tech titan announced. "So I shot him. He wasn't real anyway."

"What the hell does that mean?"

Balthazar shrugged. "This is all a simulation. I'm the only one who can't die, because I'm the main character."

"What?"

"Anyway, I didn't know him that well to begin with," Balthazar said as he used the thumb release of his rifle to eject an empty .300 Win Mag magazine, which held five rounds. He went into his kit, found a fresh magazine, and rocked it into the magazine well before chambering the first bullet.

Lance looked stunned.

"Come on," Balthazar said. "I need a new head for my trophy room back home."

CHAPTER

17

His head throbbed and every joint ached as he tried to peel himself up off the ground. Of course the fall hadn't been enough to kill him. It was just high enough to make for a very painful landing. He had come down almost sideways, executing one of the laziest-looking parachute-landing falls in history. Every paratrooper had to learn to land, for obvious reasons, but it still sucked.

No, he wasn't dead. He could tell, because it hurt really bad.

It took two attempts, but he pushed up onto his knees. Lopez tasted blood in his mouth, but it didn't appear anything was broken. From his knees, he groaned as he stood to his feet. The crossbow was still slung over his back and seemed to be in one piece.

Lopez hobbled off, again fighting for distance between himself and the hunters. He knew he had been greedy going after the hunter with his club, and he knew he had been lucky too. By rights, he should have been shot numerous times over. Some effective countersniper tactics had prevented him from being hit, but only because the hunters lacked tactical experience.

He was limping a little as he tried to jog down through the gulch he had fallen into. Somewhere behind him, not farther than fifty meters away, he heard the chirp of the South African's handheld radio breaking squelch. He couldn't make out any of the words, though.

Then another shot.

He could tell it was close, because it made a snapping sound as it whizzed right over his head.

More voices now.

Lopez ran, forcing his legs to work harder even though his entire body felt rattled, as if he had been in a car crash or a vehicle rollover. Risking a glance over his shoulder, he saw the three hunters on the edge of the cliff. One was aiming a rifle in his direction while the other two looked on.

He ducked just as he saw the muzzle flash.

* * *

Balthazar grimaced as he cracked open the bolt on his rifle. He had shot another flier, a miss that went wide of his target, who had ducked and bolted behind an embankment as the gulch turned in another direction.

"Have to check the zero on this rifle," he muttered. "Something is off with my scope."

"Your zero is fine," DeKlerk said. "You're milking the trigger, Sally."

Balthazar looked like he was about to erupt. His face went red, and DeKlerk secretly hoped the world's wealthiest man reached critical mass and said or did something irreversible, because he would love the opportunity to sink his fist into his smug face.

"Guys," Lance said from behind them. "I'm not feeling so hot."

He did look a little pale. Blood had absorbed into his shirtsleeve, dyeing it crimson. DeKlerk used his knife to cut away the sleeve, discarding it into the bushes. He then applied a medical bandage to the wound.

The crossbow bolt had sliced a nice clean line across Lance's shoulder, half an inch deep toward the center of the wound. It bled a lot but wasn't life-threatening, DeKlerk informed him.

"Just a flesh wound," Balthazar mocked. "Let's get moving before something else in the system glitches."

* * *

Lopez came to a large open area that was occupied by a large herd of elephants. About thirty of them milled about, a combination of adult females and juveniles, many of them appearing to be ten or twelve feet tall.

The tactically correct answer was to avoid large open areas where he might get shot, not to mention avoid wildlife that could trample him to death. However, he could already hear the hunters making their way down the cliff and into the gulch.

He didn't have time to find a way to skirt around.

The Ranger took a deep breath, knowing that his decisions were becoming increasingly reckless proportional to his desperation.

As he took off running into the clearing, the larger female elephants responded, turning toward him. One of them let loose what sounded like a trumpet blast from its trunk. He knew the animals were simply trying to warn him off, but he had little choice but to continue on azimuth, as it were. He didn't have many fight options left, so flight it was.

Spotting a gap between the elephants, he ran full tilt for it, even as they began to display some aggressiveness, but really they were simply trying to protect their calves. The biggest elephant, possibly the herd matriarch, stomped toward him. Now that he was closer, the Ranger saw that she was probably closer to twelve or fourteen feet tall and must weigh several tons.

Elephants were known to kill threats by stomping them to death, sometimes also goring them with their tusks.

His joints still felt like they belonged to the tin man and needed some oil, but he pressed on, speeding up, as the matriarch did not appear poised to tolerate his presence for even a few more seconds.

He passed between two juveniles that went scattering in opposite directions, seeking the protection of the larger elephants. Meanwhile, the matriarch closed on him and swung her trunk toward him. Lopez dodged, fearing he would be lifted up and thrown by the alpha female.

He stumbled, picked himself back up, and ran, now finding himself on the opposite side of the herd from where he had started. He had made it to the other side. But in the process, he had seriously pissed off the herd.

Three of the elephants charged him. He was sure their intent was to simply crush him under their massive feet.

The ground was shaking beneath his feet as he turned and ran at a dead sprint for the wood line at the edge of the clearing.

CHAPTER 18

"THAT CRAZY SON of a bitch," DeKlerk said with a touch of admiration in his voice.

"Jesus," Lance let out.

The trio had stumbled down a path that zigzagged down the cliff face and gave chase to their quarry. As they came to the clearing, it seemed that the hunting party had reached the end game. They would have a clear shot, and the Ranger had nowhere to run.

Then he'd done something completely idiotic and unexpected. He'd run right into the center of the herd of elephants in the clearing.

The three hunters held their breath, maneuvering themselves to see through gaps in the herd to see if Lopez made it to the other side. Instead, the ground shook and a cloud of dust rose as the elephants stampeded.

Lance fell to his knees while Balthazar clutched his rifle like a favored teddy bear.

"Do you see the Yank?" DeKlerk asked.

"Too much dust," Balthazar replied. "Can't see anything on the other side."

"Maybe the critters got him," DeKlerk said. "That was hectic."

"No matter," Balthazar announced as he sighted down his rifle and opened fire on the elephant herd. Splotches of blood appeared on the hide of one of the elephants as he racked the bolt and fired again and again until the herd had dispersed back into the forest.

"Stupid animals," he cursed.

DeKlerk looked at him like he was an idiot.

"Let's go look for the Yank's body. Nobody walks away from something like that."

* * *

Lopez pulled his bleeding body from a thicket of brambles. Long black thorns had torn his flesh, but he had little option but to dive into the brush headfirst or be gored and crushed to death by the elephant stampede.

Thankfully, the elephants seemed to have broken off in another direction and wandered away as opposed to chasing him into the forest.

Wincing, he pulled a thorn out of his tricep and tossed it away. He'd survived, but now he looked like the messiah in a Mel Gibson holy roller film as blood streaked down his face and arms. Once again, the pain reminded him that he was still alive.

Unslinging the crossbow, he withdrew one of the bolts from the quiver mounted under it and held the arrow in his mouth while he worked to load the bow. The string had to be withdrawn and locked in the rearward position before the arrow was put into place.

The muscles in his arms and shoulders strained as he strung the crossbow, the muscle fatigue being a sign of dehydration.

With that accomplished, he held the crossbow in his hands and made sure he was familiar with where the safety mechanism was and how it worked. His gamble had bought him some time, but he knew it was still only a matter of time before the three hunters caught up with him once again.

Maybe he could take down one of them with the crossbow, but not all three when they were firing rifles at him. Still, he felt a little better with an actual weapon in his hands. Turning, he moved back into the foliage.

* * *

"Anything?"

"No, nothing," Lance answered.

DeKlerk swore. They had searched the far end of the clearing by sweeping back and forth several times, but there was no body. He had eluded them once more.

And yet, every time he escaped the noose tightened around the American's neck just a little more. He was getting closer and closer to the blocking positions where four more hunters waited patiently to intercept him.

DeKlerk went into the wood line searching for spoor, some sign of the direction the Ranger had gone in. He found all kinds of signs around a thicket of thornbushes. It was pretty clear that the American had pulled himself through the brush and continued south.

"Let's go kill this motherfucker," Lance said.

DeKlerk grinned, glad that the injured hunter had reacquired his killer spirit.

"That way," he said, pointing.

CHAPTER

19

"REX?" HENRY CALLED out in a whisper. "What is that?"

Henry thought he had heard something in the forest, maybe a twig snapping? Rex was just ten or fifteen meters to his left, but Henry had now lost sight of him.

They had spent the entire day sweating in the woods, trying to avoid the African heat to little avail. Gideon was paired off with Gold somewhere off to their right flank to complete the anvil part of DeKlerk's hammer-and-anvil strategy. Henry was silently grateful to be away from Gold for a while due to his nonstop proselytizing.

Rex and Henry had conversed throughout the morning and into the afternoon to stave off boredom, if nothing else, but now Henry couldn't see or hear his teammate.

Henry hefted his Sako 90 rifle, chambered to fire a 6.5 Creedmoor round, and set off to find Rex, softly calling out his name. There was no reply.

He reached for his radio.

"BP One, this is BP Two, over."

"Yes?" Gold's voice crackled through the static with no regard for radio protocols.

"Do you have eyes on Rex at all?"

"No, we thought he was with you."

"So did I, but I'm not sure where he went," Henry said as he walked over to where he had last seen his partner.

"Maybe he went off to relieve himself?"

"What the fuck is going on over there?" DeKlerk's voice broke through into the radio net. "All of you stand to; the Yank is going to be at your position any second."

Henry scanned the forest ahead of him, looking over the same trees and bushes he had been staring at all day.

"Standing by," he said into his radio, unhappy with DeKlerk's uppity tone.

As he reached down to clip the radio back on his belt, he noticed a red splatter-type pattern on the grass around his feet. He looked a little closer, bent over at the waist and touched it. Rubbing his fingers together, he noticed that it looked and felt like blood.

"What the hell?" he asked himself.

Looking around the immediate vicinity, he found more blood splatter but no sign of animals. Then he walked around a tree, and in knee-high grass, he saw Rex.

He lay there in the grass, covered in blood, an arrow jutting out from his neck. His eyes looked as if they were bugging out of his skull. Henry carefully stepped forward, taking a closer look.

"Oh fuck, oh fuck, oh fuck," he gasped like a broken record.

Henry looked to see if Rex was still breathing, then tried to find a pulse. Nothing. He palmed the radio at his hip and held it up to his mouth.

"Rex is dead," he announced over the net.

"You're sure?" Gold asked. "We haven't seen anything."

"I'm pretty fucking sure. I'm standing over his body right now. He's got a crossbow bolt in his fucking neck. Where the fuck did a crossbow come from?"

"Bad news on that front, mate." DeKlerk broke into the conversation again. "The crossbow came from Wayne, who is also now dead. Sounds like the Yank already hit your BPs without you knowing it. Hold tight; we'll be at your position in a few minutes."

Henry swallowed. There was so much blood. As his pulse slowly returned to normal, he noticed something else. Rex's rifle was missing. So was the photographer's vest he had been wearing, and the canteen he wore on his hip was also gone.

The Ranger had ghosted right up to their blocking position, murdered Rex, and stripped his body before pulling a fade.

CHAPTER

20

LOPEZ CREPT BEHIND a boulder and used it as cover to take stock of his situation as he dumped the gear he had been carrying in his arms at his feet.

Minutes prior he had been stalking through the forest and come upon the first of the blocking positions he had expected to eventually find since he'd first heard the helicopter in the morning. Through the tree leaves and tall grass, he spotted one of the hunters wearing his L.L.Bean starter set.

He was already close enough, and the arrow would certainly fire with enough force to break through the thick foliage and strike his target beyond. Using the crossbow's scope, he lined up the cross hairs center mass and gently stroked the trigger.

The crossbow made a muted snapping sound as the arrow launched forward, and his target went down in a shower of blood that spurted from the wound. Lopez quickly closed the distance and wasted no time. He knew there were at least three other hunters in the vicinity.

Quickly, efficiently, and with the same callous disregard for life and death that the hunters had shown him, he stripped the body of useful items. He claimed a Sako bolt-action rifle and a canteen, then yanked off the hunter's safari photographer vest and shrugged it over his shoulders.

With the rifle in his hand, he turned as he heard someone pass right behind him. For a split second he saw the one with the dirty-blond hair, recognizing him from the previous day. But just as soon as he saw the hunter, he was gone. He had run right past Lopez and Rex's body completely unaware.

Knowing he was trying his luck, Lopez saw one final item to strip from the body before moving on. He grabbed Rex's walkie-talkie radio and disappeared into the forest.

Now, with some temporary safety, he listened to the remaining hunters frantically communicate with one another over the radio while he drank greedily from the canteen. Downing almost all the water, he slung the crossbow over his back and rested the rifle against the boulder. Then he quickly began feeling through the pockets in the vest.

In one of them, he found a Clif Bar. It was a high-calorie oat-and-brown-rice-based bar made for athletes and outdoorsmen to eat on the go.

Tearing off the wrapper, he shoved half of it in his mouth and began to chew. He hadn't eaten in a couple of days, and the lack of fuel for his body under the African sun was wearing on him almost as much as the dehydration.

He was going to turn the tables on these motherfuckers. One by one. There was no way he was going to let Wallaby down. He'd find a way to get his teammate back, one way or the other.

As he swallowed down the rest of the energy bar, he rummaged through the other pockets, finding a nicotine vape pen, another Clif Bar, a small compass, a pocketknife, and crammed into one pocket, even a tourniquet and medical bandage that the hunter would never need now that he had an arrow sticking through his neck.

All things considered, it wasn't much, but he was now in a far better position than he had been in the morning.

The enemy had been reduced from eight to six, and now Lopez was armed with a crossbow and a bolt-action hunting rifle. He even had a small stash of food and water, at least enough to keep him going a little while longer. He could take some comfort in that at least. There was a saying he remembered from SERE school about maintaining a positive outlook during such situations.

"Small victories," he whispered under his breath.

Then there was the radio. Lopez lowered the volume knob and then clicked it on to begin listening.

* * *

Henry's face was still ashen when DeKlerk, Lance, and Balthazar caught up with him. A few moments later, Gold and Gideon came crashing through the forest. Together they stood in a semicircle around Rex's body, gawking at it.

"That fucking scumbag," Henry cursed. "I can't fucking believe this."

"What do you mean, you can't believe it?" Balthazar retorted. "We're hunting him like a wild animal, so of course he's going to behave like one."

"Rex was a titan of the defense industry, the real-life Tony Stark," Henry complained. "What right does that rat have to kill him?"

Balthazar rolled his eyes; after all, he thought, none of this was real. "Rex got complacent and paid the price. Wayne too."

"DeKlerk," Gideon said, his thin lips barely moving as he spoke. "This wasn't part of the game plan."

"You wanted to hunt the most dangerous game. When you got tired of shooting poachers, you requested that I find you more cunning prey. This is literally what you've paid me to do," the South African said.

"Do you have any idea what those two men were to our future plans in America?"

"No, I don't," DeKlerk answered candidly. "Nor do I care about your plans. Once again, that's not what you paid me for."

"In our medieval past, even monarchs died on hunting expeditions," Gold interjected, carrying on his homily. "The fact that they died means we can experience the authentic exhilaration of hunting and killing. You know, during the Spanish Civil War, landowners would sometimes hunt landless peasants for sport. They called it *agrarian reform* in reference to the mass graves they filled."

Gideon, Balthazar, Henry, and Lance traded looks.

"Sun will be down in another hour," DeKlerk said, breaking the silence. "Better find camp."

CHAPTER

21

LOPEZ FOUND AN area thick with brush as the sun began to sink below the horizon. He cleared a way into the center of the brush to where there was a small overturned tree, its roots sticking into the air and leaving a ditch where it had fallen.

Scouting around, he found some more deadfall and laid it across the downed tree, making an improvised shelter. He then pulled up some of the greener brush and laid it over the top as some hasty camouflage.

He next chugged down the rest of the water in his newly liberated canteen and huffed down the second Clif Bar. They were the only spoils of war he was going to get.

Lopez was pushing all his training and experience to the limit in search of any advantage at all. He was arguably one of the best-trained soldiers in the United States military, but even he was hitting a wall at this point. Africa was quite harsh.

Thinking it through, though, he did have a lot to fall back on. Not just his training but also his unit's history.

The 75th Ranger Regiment was itself a special operations outfit, an elite unit of paratroopers who were on call 24-7 to respond to contingency scenarios and crises worldwide. However, it also hid a smaller, even more elite unit, of which he was a part.

That unit had started up in 1984 and was called the Regimental Reconnaissance Detachment, or RRD. It consisted at that time of just three teams, which ran recon for the three infantry battalions in the Ranger Regiment. Back in those early days, RRD's main job was to conduct recon for airfield seizures.

A six-man RRD team would free-fall days ahead of the main element, place an airfield under observation, locate enemy positions, and radio back to headquarters what they saw before the Ranger battalion came in and did a static line jump right over the airfield itself.

The unit evolved over the years and was brought into the special operations task force that was hunting war criminals in the Balkans during the 1990s, usually teamed up with Delta Force operators. This was also the time that RRD began abandoning their distinctive "high and tight" Ranger haircuts in order to blend in better. In 1997, during a joint readiness exercise, their Ranger haircuts were considered an operational security—OPSEC—violation. Those haircuts precluded them from being able to fly on "covered" aircraft, that is, nonstandard aircraft disguised as civilian aviation. To stay relevant, RRD had to ditch the high and tight.

After 9/11, RRD morphed into RRC, expanding into a company that now had six teams instead of three. Those recon Rangers did combat free-fall jumps in Afghanistan and conducted recon to support Ranger and JSOC targets. During the Iraq invasion, they augmented the Delta Force and were involved in some large-scale contacts with Saddam's forces.

That was all in the past, Ranger lore that Lopez had heard about from the old-timers. By the time he got to RRC, they were doing Omega Team deployments and then later running the Afghan Reconnaissance Unit, or ARU. Nowadays, RRC was often "one up" or "two up" for an entire country, deploying singletons or pairs of guys to run all ops there. Other times they were paired with a Delta operator and a guy from Titan Zeus who did signals intel, making them a three-man team.

Today, RRC made up a part of JSOC's intel and recon community. There were four tactical recon elements in JSOC: Delta's G Squadron, SEAL Team Six's Black Squadron, the 75th's Regimental Recon Company, and Titan Zeus, or TZ, better known as Intelligence Support Activity or Task Force Orange, which was the unit Wallaby served in.

Simply to serve in the Ranger Regiment required passing the Ranger Assessment and Selection Program, or RASP, and despite Lopez being a fairly seasoned Ranger, he'd still had to complete RRC's own selection course held in Dahlonega, Georgia.

It was weeks of grueling land navigation up and down the mountains with a heavy rucksack on his back. Toward the end, he and his fellow Rangers spent some time in town being assessed on some very basic tradecraft, like servicing dead drop locations. Finally, there was an interview with a military psychologist, and then he went before a selection board made up of RRC veterans and other Ranger leaders.

Once selected, he then went right into the Recon Training Course, or RTC. This included training on advanced radio operations, conducting tactical recon training missions, constructing hide sites, using high-powered optics and photography equipment for observation, advanced spy tradecraft, advanced marksmanship training, and military free-fall operations.

Since Lopez had been in the unit, he had also graduated from the Special Forces Sniper Course on Fort Bragg and from RSLC, the Recon and Surveillance Leader's Course, on Fort Benning. His team had also cross-trained him as a medic in addition to his normal duties, which usually consisted of walking as point man for Team Three.

He'd need every single lesson learned, every aspect of his training, to push himself to the max if he intended to survive the situation he now found himself in.

There was still a bit of time before sundown, and despite his joints aching like an old man and his arms and face being covered in a combination of dried mud and blood, he was too wound up from running for his life all day to sit still. Reaching for some more downed branches and sticks, he began sharpening them into spears, not even sure why just yet when he had actual weapons.

And he remembered. He remembered that his worst day evading the enemy in the field was preferable to his best day in captivity, assuming he lived that long.

While he worked, he set the walkie-talkie radio next to him. He had barely heard a peep over the net since he turned it on. That told him something in and of itself.

Either they had switched channels or stopped using the radio entirely because they knew he had one as well, or the entire hunting party had consolidated and was now colocated somewhere to make camp.

As he worked, the gears in his head spun.

* * *

DeKlerk selected the campsite but demanded noise and light discipline. The Yank could be out there with a scoped rifle sighting in on them, for all they knew. They had their tents set up in a semicircle, which DeKlerk had them cover with cut foliage from the forest to conceal their position.

There was no denying it at this point: The hunting party had lost the overwhelming advantage they'd begun the hunt with. DeKlerk could feel it all around the camp. After three of their mates had been killed, the rich and famous were becoming the tired and the restless.

"How did that piece of shit get the drop on Rex?" Lance asked as they sat around, snacking in the darkness.

"I've played it back in my mind over and over," Henry said. "I don't understand how that guy snuck right past me."

"Don't underestimate a wild animal that has been cornered," DeKlerk advised. "He's resourceful and ruthless, because we've given him no other choice."

"What a normie twat," Balthazar said. "Who cares who he is or if his feelings are hurt? We just need to run him down, kill him, and get his head for my taxidermist back in Austin. It will look good up there on the wall next to the big five and a few poachers we retired."

Balthazar was known to maintain an extensive compound in Texas, which included his doomsday bunker but was also where he housed his baby mommas. There were at least a half dozen of them, whom he kept impregnated as much as possible, artificially or otherwise.

As a high-status male and the main character of his simulated world, he felt it was his job to create as many new versions of himself as possible. His mission was to populate the world in his image.

DeKlerk was silent. He had assessed Balthazar as the kind of guy who would have been killed by his own men during a war.

"It's fucking bullshit," Henry said. "Fucking bullshit. Fuck that dude."

Gold was busy writing something down in his journal. He seemed the most nonchalant of the group, enjoying the hunting trip as a vigorous outdoor experience.

DeKlerk assessed Gold as the type of guy who, in war, would be running around wearing an ear necklace.

The group turned as they heard a hiss of static.

"Shit," Lance said. "I forgot about my radio."

"Turn that off," DeKlerk scolded. "I said to maintain noise discipline in camp tonight."

As Lance walked over to his tent and picked up his radio, a voice broke through the static and said an unmistakable name.

"DeKlerk."

The camp froze in place. The South African looked over at Lance and squinted.

"DeKlerk, I know you're there," said the voice on the radio.

"Give that here," DeKlerk told Lance.

"DeKlerk, it's your pal Lopez on the line. Call 1–900–"

The South African grabbed the radio away from Lance.

"I hear you, Yank," DeKlerk said as he took the radio and depressed the push-to-talk button. "How's your day been going, boet?"

Boet, pronounced *boot*, was South African slang for buddy.

There was a pause as static hissed over the net.

"Good to hear from you, DeKlerk," Lopez said. The American spoke with a Southern accent that the South African could barely understand. "I'd say today went pretty well. Managed to even the odds a bit, don't you think?"

"How the fuck does he know my name?" DeKlerk asked no one in particular. The entire camp was glued to the conversation. "Can't deny you that," DeKlerk said into the radio. "You got yourself kitted out today too."

"Yup," Lopez replied. "That must have been surprising. I reckon you thought to do me in today."

"There is always tomorrow, Yank."

"I'm sure it will be an interesting one. I'm planning to show your crew a few things they've never seen before—namely, the inside of themselves."

Henry and Gideon were up on their feet now, seething with rage. DeKlerk wasn't about to let their prey get under his skin, though, as that was clearly the point. He was a wizened old mercenary, but these wealthy fuckers had paper-thin skin.

"Don't be so sure. You're still outnumbered and outgunned."

"There were eight; now there are six. How many will there be left at your camp tomorrow night?"

"Fucking scumbag. I'll flay him alive," Henry snarled.

DeKlerk held up a hand to hush him. "Well, what do you reckon, Yank?"

There was only silence.

"Lopez, you there?"

But he wasn't. Nothing but static came over the radio net.

CHAPTER 22

DEKLERK HAD THE hunting party up at the ass crack of dawn, breaking down the camp and preparing to move out. With the sun just creeping into the sky, the South African had them moving out in a modified tracking formation.

Normally, a tracking patrol would feature a tracker with a right and left flank tracker to either side, forming a Y shape. Behind the center tracker would be the controller who led the patrol. That was a military formation, though, and in this case DeKlerk led the way as the main tracker with the hunters in a single-file line behind him.

The previous night he had done a map reconnaissance and selected some likely areas where the American would bed down for the night. It was highly unlikely that he had continued on the move through the night, as it got so dark it became impossible to see in the forest.

They swept through a couple of nearby sites, guns at the ready. DeKlerk directed them to a small hill that afforded some amount of high ground, then a draw overgrown with vegetation, in search of the Ranger. Neither yielded any sign of him.

DeKlerk then focused on what appeared to be another area denser than the rest of the forest that was more or less on the American's assumed direction of travel. As they got closer, he had the hunting party shake out in an assault line and sweep forward with about five meters of spacing between each man and the next, their rifles held at the ready.

They broke brush, snapping sticks and rustling foliage, as they searched the area. At first it looked like another dry hole, but then Gideon spotted something. DeKlerk came over for a closer look, and indeed, he had found a sort of lean-to constructed from branches and sticks.

As they continued to sweep forward, it became clear that the site had been abandoned, but only recently. DeKlerk ran his hand under the lean-to and felt the depressions in the earth where the Ranger had lain down during the night. He had left the hide site perhaps just an hour ago. Maybe less. DeKlerk began searching for spoor and soon found footprints leading away, continuing south.

Then he froze in place. Up ahead it looked like a vine had been strung across the spoor trail. While Lopez was clearly not as experienced as DeKlerk at tracking and countertracking, some basic training had been in evidence thus far. Lopez also had demonstrated a habit of doglegging back on his own spoor to set up ambushes.

It appeared that he might have done so again, setting up some sort of booby trap on his own trail.

Crouched down, DeKlerk looked to the left and right of the trail until he saw something that looked out of place near the spoor. Something sharp and pointy.

"That's Wayne's crossbow," Lance said as he stepped forward. "If he was going to make a trap, he could have hid it a bit better."

"Wait—" DeKlerk started a moment too late.

Lance rushed forward toward the crossbow, and as he stepped to the side of the weapon, suddenly his feet sank into the earth up to his knees.

Lance screamed.

* * *

Lopez heard a scream somewhere behind him and smiled.

He'd slept only a few hours, but it had been worth it. He spent most of the night and into the morning constructing a punji stick trap, complete with a decoy.

The crossbow he'd left angled toward his own spoor trail, and the improvised fake trip wire he'd made with a vine torn from a tree was the decoy to bait them into the trap. The real trap was a hole dug next to the crossbow, which he had filled with sharp sticks and two of the three remaining razor-sharp steel arrows.

He'd then covered the pit over with some small sticks, then laid some brush over that. A punji stick trap was one of the oldest tricks in the guerrilla warfare book. Relatively easy to construct, such traps had been used extensively against American soldiers by the Viet Cong during the Vietnam War.

Clearly, at least one of the hunting party had taken the bait and sunk into the trap.

He continued on for another hour, grateful to have the hunting party off his back for a while. What he was looking for was a hide site from which he could initiate a long-range sniper engagement with his newly acquired rifle.

Standoff distance was usually the key determining factor behind who won a battle; in other words, how far away could you be and hurt the enemy without them yet being able to hurt you? The sniper rifle gave him much greater reach, and he was sure he was a better marksman than most of the hunters.

Then he stumbled upon something unexpected.

The forest gave way to an area that had been cut and logged. A few hundred meters away stood a small West African village. He could see huts with straw roofs and some kids playing with a soccer ball. Terra-cotta–colored structures spread over a few kilometers dotted the landscape, each appearing to have a small garden fenced in with chicken wire.

Lopez hadn't expected to find any signs of human habitation out this far, but here it was.

A sense of relief washed over him for a moment. People who weren't trying to kill him. Maybe they could even help him? A village probably meant at least one truck, at least one working cellular phone, not to mention a well for water. He broke into the clearing and began jogging toward the village.

* * *

"FUCK FUCK FUCK!"

Lance would not shut the fuck up, but the others conceded that they might not either if they had been skewered by a punji pit. Lance had fixated on the crossbow without checking his surroundings and fallen right into a punji pit trap.

DeKlerk pulled him free and began tending to his wounds. He used a pair of medical shears to cut through his boots and pant legs. They were grisly wounds but nothing the South African hadn't seen before. Both of the health insurance CEO's feet had been punctured by arrows and sharp sticks placed at the bottom of the pit.

"GOD, THAT FUCKING ASSHOLE! FUCK THIS PLACE, FUCK THIS PLACE!"

Balthazar looked annoyed by Lance's outbursts and reached into his pocket, producing a blue lozenge.

"Take this," he said to Lance.

Lance hesitated, his mind drifting to yesterday when Balthazar had put Wayne out of his misery. Maybe that had been a mercy kill, but Lance's wounds were probably not life-threatening. Why was Balthazar still playing Dr. Kevorkian? The bastard seemed to enjoy the role a little too much.

"Relax," Balthazar said. "It's just ketamine. I've been microdosing these for years. It will help with the pain."

Cautiously, Lance reached for the pill.

"Put it under your tongue and hold it there. You'll start feeling better soon."

DeKlerk finished bandaging the wounds to the best of his ability in a field setting.

"We're going to have to call in the heli," DeKlerk announced.

"Is there a hospital that the pilot can fly him to?" Gideon asked.

"Not in a timely manner," DeKlerk said. "Besides, I have other plans. We're not finished with you yet, Lance. We're going to need your assistance for what comes next."

Reaching into his pack, the South African produced a larger radio than their walkie-talkies and raised up a long whip antenna to begin hailing the helicopter pilot.

CHAPTER 23

WHEN LOPEZ ENTERED the village, even with a rifle slung over his shoulder, he was instantly swarmed by children shouting in a language he didn't understand.

But they weren't angry; they were smiling, laughing, and calling out to him. They seemed excited to see a stranger in their remote part of the world. Lopez smiled back, happier to see them than they ever could have known.

"Does anyone here speak English?" Lopez asked them hopefully. "Or maybe Spanglish?" He also spoke a little bit of Pashto, but that seemed unlikely to be helpful in this scenario.

A few minutes later, some of the adults began showing themselves, drawn by the sudden commotion caused by the children. He didn't understand what they were saying, but they began patting him on the shoulder and led him to a water cistern on top of one of the huts. They were trying to help him.

When he thumbed a small metal lever, rainwater ran out of the spigot and right into Lopez's mouth. He downed as much water as he could before filling his canteen. Then he let the water run over his face and scrubbed free the dried mud and blood that he had not sweated off already. Despite the heat, the water was ice cold.

"American?"

Lopez turned to the voice and saw a skinny kid who couldn't have been older than thirteen.

"English?" he asked.

"Yeah, bro," the kid answered.

Lopez grinned.

"Where did you learn English, kid?"

"USA TV shows."

Lopez shook his head. It was the same the world over.

"You know Taylor Swift?"

"Of course I know Taylor Swift."

American pop culture coming through for him. For some reason he was reminded of being in a Ranger platoon in Afghanistan, where they had blasted Taylor Swift songs in their gear load-out room before missions.

"Do your parents speak English too?"

The boy laughed at him. "I the only one. What your name?"

"Jeremy."

"Jeremy what? You have other name?"

"Jeremy Lopez."

The boy laughed again.

"You J-Lo!" the boy laughed. "Hey, Jenny from the block!"

Lopez rubbed his forehead. He'd only been hearing that joke his entire life, mostly from his Ranger teammates. Apparently he wasn't exempt even in the most austere parts of Africa.

"What's your name?"

"Geraud."

"All right then."

"Your sister very beautiful."

"She's not my sister, kid."

Suddenly, there was a commotion outside. Villagers were running and screaming. Lopez scooped up his rifle and scanned the area, surprised that the hunting party had caught up with him so fast. It didn't seem probable or even possible.

As he walked into the center of the village, Lopez realized that the hunters had not arrived, but in the distance a cloud of dust rose into the cloudless blue sky, scaring the villagers. They must know who was coming, he concluded.

Women were running, grabbing their children, some of them even taking their kids and running into the wood line.

Through the scope on his rifle, Lopez looked at the approaching dust cloud. There were two Toyota pickup trucks heading straight for the village.

"Who the fuck is that?"

"Bad guys," the kid answered matter-of-factly.

"Bandits?"

"Yeah, they come. Take women."

Lopez lowered his rifle and gritted his teeth. He turned toward the kid. "Not today they're not."

CHAPTER 24

FROM THE COUNTRY brief he'd been given when he deployed to Niger, Lopez recalled that there was a loose coalition of Al Qaeda–aligned Islamic terrorist organizations that operated in the Sahel, including along the border regions between Niger, Burkina Faso, and Benin.

When he asked, the boy informed him that they were in Benin, which was good to know, if not particularly helpful at the moment.

Families that had not fled into the forest were barring their doors, shuttering windows, and preparing for the worst. Clearly, this wasn't their first run-in with the terrorists.

Lopez clenched his jaw. He understood combat, and killing the enemy on the battlefield was just business as far as he was concerned. It wasn't necessarily a personal thing. But this was different. The Ranger had no time for the worst kind of scum, the kind that victimized women and children.

"Go inside, kid," Lopez told his teenage interlocutor. "Don't come out until the shooting stops."

"What you gonna do, J-Lo?"

Lopez considered his options. He had five rounds in the rifle's internal magazine and another five laced into the elastic banding on the stock of his rifle. Ten shots for two truckloads of bandits.

"Go inside," he repeated. "I'm gonna kill them."

* * *

There were about two dozen huts in the village, just about all of them associated with a small garden adjacent to them. The walls were largely constructed of mud and the roofs made of thatch. A single dirt road running east to west bifurcated the village.

The two-vehicle convoy would reach the village in less than a minute, leaving Lopez without time to organize a complex ambush. He assessed that his best chance would come from a shock-and-awe campaign. Surprise, speed, and violence of action were the key elements.

Holding the rifle at port arms, he moved deeper into the village, away from the road, to find a position that offered cover and concealment.

Lopez headed deeper into the village as Geraud made off in the other direction. Looping around the outskirts of the town—running alongside dirt walls, vaulting over a few chicken-wire fences around outdoor gardens, and ducking under a clothesline—he maneuvered to a position where he could overwatch the road leading into the village. Just as the convoy reached the first of the huts, he took up a position using one of the mud walls for partial cover.

The two pickup trucks ground to a halt a hundred meters away in a cloud of the ubiquitous orange dust that characterized the region. Men began jumping out of the bed of the truck and opening the doors while shouting. They wore chest rigs filled with spare magazines and carried an assortment of AK-47s, RPKs, and even a few M16s that they'd probably taken off dead local security forces.

Lopez was going to see what he could do about recovering them.

Exhausted, dehydrated, starved, and hunted, Lopez felt every painful distraction suddenly slip away as he aligned his cross hairs on the enemy. Black walls closed in and shrouded his focus from the outside world. His finger slowly wound its way into the trigger guard and gently touched the trigger. His breathing was slow, rhythmic, as years of sniper training took over.

For a brief second, the world made sense to him. He had entered into a meditative state.

The trigger broke and the first target went down in an aerosol spray of blood. Working from muscle memory, Lopez worked the Sako rifle's bolt, ejecting a hot 6.5 brass shell casing and loading the next round from the internal magazine. Up on one knee, his tricep braced against the other knee for stability, he was able to quickly transition targets by making the slightest movements with his arms and legs.

The trigger broke a second time as his sights came across the next terrorist, spinning him and depositing him on the ground in another cloud of dust.

Lopez racked the bolt, shifting his weight until the next target showed front and center in his scope. The Ranger could see the look of confusion on the terrorist's face as he gently squeezed the trigger. As the bullet impacted, Lopez was already working the bolt again, watching his target fall backward over a knee-high stone wall. He lay where he fell, his sandaled feet hanging over the wall.

The next gunman near the wall looked down at his fallen comrade, clearly surprised, but not for long. Lopez shifted his point of aim again. Having turned to look at his dead buddy, the terrorist was now presenting him with a slightly smaller target, but he was still only a hundred meters away. Lopez put his point of aim under the terrorist's armpit. When he stroked the trigger, the round blasted through his target's rib cage and ruptured both his lungs. He collapsed and lay still next to his buddy.

Lopez ejected the spent brass, sending it spinning end over end. It bounced off the mud wall and fell at his feet.

Another terrorist ran from behind the hood of the first pickup and leveled his Kalashnikov in Lopez's general direction. They both fired their weapons simultaneously. The terrorist's shot went wide; Lopez's shot didn't. It struck a bit above his point of aim, taking his target in the neck. The terrorist fell backward, bending at the knees, and died in an unnatural position with his lower legs bent and trapped underneath him.

Lopez ejected the brass and was now on an empty chamber. No more quarters in that video game. He needed to reload.

Miniature clouds of dust sprouting up around him and the familiar snap of rounds screaming through the air over his head told Lopez he was now taking effective fire. Pushing off with one foot, he stayed low and near the wall as he began running for a new position.

He had only five shots left, and there looked to be twice that many gunmen left. He had seized the initiative and racked up some kills, but at this point the odds were against him. He was both outmanned and outgunned.

Again. This had been the third time within a week that he had been backed into a corner like this. He couldn't quite claim to like the experience, but it did have a way of focusing your priorities. Survival was the final and ultimate goal. By comparison, nothing else—like not doing your income taxes or hanging your flag on the porch on Memorial Day—really mattered. Folks back home would never really understand what he knew.

While still on the move, he cradled the Sako hunting rifle in his left arm and reloaded with his right hand, snatching 6.5 Creedmoor rounds from the elastic holders on the buttstock and pressing them down into the internal magazine, where they snapped into place.

Slamming the bolt shut, Lopez pivoted and headed back for the road.

Coming around another corner, he saw several other terrorists milling around the vehicles and barking orders. He was about two hundred meters away at this point. He braced himself against the wall of another mud hut for stabilization and let his cross hairs fall on the nearest gunman. When the terrorist turned and presented his chest, Lopez squeezed the trigger.

He gained target acquisition on the next terrorist before the first had hit the ground. This one was now running toward him with two others in tow. In the parallax of his scope, Lopez noticed something and quickly changed targets. Alongside one of the houses was a white propane bottle that the local villagers normally used for cooking.

Lopez squeezed the trigger and saw a spark on the tank for a split second when his round made contact, and then the flammable gas burst out in a fiery explosion that temporarily engulfed two of the three terrorists. They spun wildly, attempting to put out the flames burning their clothes. The third terrorist had not been lit ablaze, but he looked confused until Lopez loaded the next round into his rifle and killed him.

He had two shots left.

Just then autofire raked his position, coming from behind, forcing Lopez around the corner and out onto the road. He hadn't clocked a belt-fed machine gun among the group of terrorists when they pulled up, but then, he hadn't had a good view of all of them. Clearly, a group had chased after him and caught up.

Lopez quickly crossed the street and jumped over a low wall into a garden. On the road he was open to fire from two angles, some of it already coming his way, and he needed to escape that area as soon as possible.

Chancing a glance over the wall, he saw a group of about a half dozen terrorists moving through the alleyway between two huts. Meanwhile, the two terrorists he had set on fire were literally smoldering as they made their way up the road toward him, firing randomly in the process.

The wall he had as cover was only a few feet high, and now he was caught in a pincer attack. If he broke cover and ran, there was little doubt he'd be cut down. Whatever the case, he had little option but to take down as many of the enemy as he could.

Leveling his sniper rifle, Lopez flinched as a round snapped just over his head. He could physically feel it breeze past his ear.

Ignoring the danger, he elevated himself just over the lip of the wall and cracked off a shot that took down the PKM machine gunner, who was now less than fifty meters away. The terrorist depressed the trigger as he fell backward, the staccato burst of autofire sweeping across a mud wall and also taking out one of his buddies in the process, whose blood and gore splattered on the wall beside him.

Lopez racked the bolt and loaded his last round.

One of the smoldering terrorists that had escaped the explosion came running down the street, firing his AK on automatic, the rounds spilling from the barrel in random directions as he closed on Lopez. The Ranger shouldered his rifle and sent his last bullet center mass into the terrorist's chest. The target took two more steps, then pitched forward and landed face-first on the dirt road.

Discarding the now-useless rifle, Lopez made to move into a crouching run and make a break for it but was immediately driven back down into the vegetable garden by rapid gunfire. One of the other terrorists must have taken control of the PKM and was sending 7.62×54R armor-piercing incendiary rounds downrange, chewing apart the knee-high wall he had taken cover behind.

He was trapped, and also, he was fucked.

Lopez turned and gripped the rifle again, preparing to use it as a club.

A new feeling rushed over him, one of relief. He didn't mind if he died doing this, defending women and children from terrorists.

This would be a good death. *It is what it is,* he thought. He had made peace with the knowledge that this day was coming for him many years ago.

CHAPTER

25

LOPEZ GRIPPED THE rifle barrel in two hands, ready to swing it and buttstroke the first terrorist that tried to come over the wall. He would be ventilated by gunfire at that point, but so fucking what?

He heard the voices getting closer, one of them barking orders.

His knuckles went white as he clenched down on the gun barrel. He planted one foot on the ground, preparing to spring forward with as much momentum as possible. The closest terrorist, the one barking orders, came into view, and for no more than a nanosecond, they locked eyes.

Lopez swung, and the whole world erupted in gunfire.

He felt the rifle stock make contact with the side of the terrorist's head, but gunfire was suddenly all around him, seemingly from every direction. The momentum of the rifle carried him forward, and he stumbled over the wall. Amazed that he wasn't dead yet, he looked up and saw the corpses of several dead terrorists and several more running away.

Then he heard voices shouting in the indigenous language as villagers came up alongside him at the wall. Geraud was suddenly at his side, an ancient rusted shotgun in his hands. The wooden stock looked as if it had been eaten away by termites or worms.

Cracking open the breech, the teenager loaded two more shells into the antique. A handful of other villagers shot at their would-be oppressors with SKS and Mosin-Nagant rifles that also appeared to be of ancient vintage.

Another terrorist went down under the barrage; two more were stumbling away wounded as the villagers broke cover and gave chase.

Lopez let go of the rifle still clenched in his grip. He was struggling to catch his breath and braced himself with both hands against the wall.

"You take big risk, J-Lo," Geraud said from behind him.

"Thanks, kid."

Lopez ran his hand across his face, wiping off some of the sweat. His hand was vibrating slightly as his body bled off the adrenaline that had flooded his veins over the last few minutes. The village had risen up, freeing themselves and saving him in the process.

"After you go, I told the others you were going to fight. They went home and got their guns."

"I'd be dead if you hadn't."

"We would die if you hadn't."

Lopez nodded and looked away.

He wasn't good with emotions. The villagers had risked everything for him, because he was willing to do the same.

Then he heard the helicopter off in the distance, the beat of its rotor blades growing closer.

"For fuck's sake," Lopez said under his breath.

Stepping over the wall, he stripped one of the terrorists of his chest rig and then began taking Kalashnikov magazines from the other dead fighters, stuffing them into the mag pouches in the chest rig and, when that was full, his pockets.

He went looking for a serviceable AK and found one that was older, but older meant it had a receiver that had been milled out of a solid piece of billet rather than being made out of stamped metal. Moving the selector all the way down for single shots, he fired a few rounds into the dirt to test fire the rifle. It passed the functions check.

Sure enough, the stamp on the receiver, a commie five-point star, signaled that the rifle had been made several lifetimes ago in the Soviet Union.

"You better get going, kid," Lopez said to Geraud. "For real this time. Go indoors; don't come out until you can't hear that helicopter anymore." He pointed to the sky.

"More bad men?"

"Total assholes."

"Next time you give me your sister number," Geraud said, flashing a white toothy grin as he turned and ran.

"She's not—" Lopez began, before giving up and smiling as the kid disappeared from view.

Lopez turned and jogged down to the pickups. Both of them were pretty shot full of holes, but he chose the one with the key still in the ignition because he didn't have a choice. There was no time to try to hot-wire a vehicle anyway.

He needed to lead the hunting party away from the village before the locals ended up as collateral damage by being caught in the cross fire. They had already experienced enough violence today.

When he turned the key, the Hilux started right up. Lopez put it into gear, backed up, and started out of the village just as the helicopter was arriving. The blue-and-white Bell helicopter buzzed over the roofs of the village, veered away right over Lopez's vehicle, and then swooped back around the village. They had seen the truck leaving but wanted to do another fly-by to see what they could. No doubt they'd notice the couple dozen corpses he had left in his wake.

He continued shifting gears and increasing speed, seeking to escape the village as quickly as possible, knowing that it would ultimately be futile. He wasn't going to outpace a helicopter in his beater Toyota pickup.

Sure enough, he soon heard the rotor blades once more and even spotted the shadow cast by the bird off to his left-hand side. They were quickly gaining on him.

Without any further warning, a bullet hole popped into the hood of his truck. Someone was shooting from the helicopter. Lopez jerked the wheel, attempting to evade, but the windshield exploded into thousands of tiny shards of glass.

CHAPTER

26

DEKLERK LED THE way into the village with Balthazar, Henry, Gideon, and Gold trailing behind him.

Balthazar kicked at one of the corpses as they passed. The hunters had spent the afternoon in the wood line watching the village through their scoped hunting rifles, doing their best to keep tabs on Lopez while they called the helicopter in.

Then there was a firefight. They had a front-row seat to Lopez smoke-checking about a dozen militants, which the entire crew had to admit was pretty impressive. Last they heard, Lopez had commandeered a vehicle and was being chased down by the helicopter.

Balthazar reached down and grabbed the dead villager by the ear and drew his knife. He was about to cut a war trophy off when DeKlerk told him to get a move on. Balthazar couldn't hold his horses, so he shot several of the villagers who had been fleeing toward the jungle to escape the raiding party. It was just for fun. In his mind, none of them were real people anyway; the simulation's nonplayer characters were inserted into the programming purely for his entertainment. The world was his plaything. Why shouldn't he have an ear collection?

DeKlerk walked into the center of the village and looked over the corpses of the dead terrorists. An expert tracker, he knew how to read the scene of a firefight.

"They pinned him down there by the wall," the old mercenary informed the hunting party. "He was penned in from two sides, you see."

Balthazar dejectedly kicked at the expended brass on the ground.

"Looks like he took down most of them and then got some help from the villagers," DeKlerk said as he picked up several green-colored shotgun shell casings.

"You sure he's not a Navy SEAL?" Henry asked.

"Or a Marine?" Gideon added.

"Apparently not," DeKlerk said. "Interesting Yank, that one. You know, when you take away their night vision, their air support, and all their high-tech toys, I did not think an American would be good in the woods. In this case, that wasn't true. This one knows how to put up a fight."

But there was something more than that, more than what he would say aloud. The old mercenary actually felt something. The young Ranger had inspired the villagers to rise up. The Ranger had leadership abilities he didn't even realize he possessed.

The radio on his hip crackled.

"We got eyes on him," the helicopter pilot said over the net. "Engaging now."

"You think Lance will tag him?" Henry asked.

"I hope so. He certainly has enough drugs in him to kill a horse by now," Balthazar replied.

* * *

Lance was pumped. The straps anchoring him to the interior of the helicopter held as he leaned out the open side door, the forest rushing past him in a brilliant blur of light. He was deep into his K-hole, a ketamine high the likes of which he had never experienced before.

In his head he sang along to an old Stevie Nicks song, his auditory hallucinations vibing right along with the floating jellyfish shapes that he saw breezing across his field of vision.

"There he is," the pilot said over the headset he wore.

Lance racked a round into his hunting rifle as the pilot maneuvered alongside the Toyota pickup truck that Lopez was attempting to escape in. He wasn't going to get much of anywhere on one tank of gas anyhow because of how far out they were, but the Ranger didn't know that.

The pilot had pulled them up alongside the truck as it peeled down the road, leaving a plume of dust behind it. The helicopter was about twenty-five meters away from the left side of the truck and about ten meters off the deck.

Shooting from a moving aerial platform such as a helicopter was a challenge for even the most seasoned of snipers, and Lance was not one of them.

He attempted to look down his scope and found himself swimming mentally as everything in his sights oscillated in all directions. Thinking he had the truck somewhat in his cross hairs, he cranked off a round. Looking up, he saw that his bullet had blasted into the hood of the truck rather than at the driver.

"Fuck," he cursed as he jacked another round into the chamber.

Suddenly, he remembered that he could reduce the magnification on the scope by turning a dial, which backed it off from 10x to just 3.5x magnification. His vision was still swirling and the hallucinations weren't helping, but damn he felt good.

As they flew, he felt disassociated from his own body, as if he were flying through the air himself. He was ready to blast off. Ready to commune with the lizard people and the giant insects who oversaw the ancient mysteries of the universe.

He cranked off another round, and the pickup truck's windshield exploded into a shower of glass cubes that glinted in the sun as they dispersed.

Lopez spun the wheel, and the vehicle turned off the road toward the helicopter, getting under them in a few seconds. The hard-packed earth facilitated off-road driving as long as you could avoid most of the shrubs and trees in the savanna.

As the helicopter looped around to reacquire their target, Lance could see where Lopez was heading. He was driving straight toward the wood line, trying to get back into the forest. He knew that out on the open road, he was basically a sitting duck.

The Ranger was dodging between the bushes and scattered trees as he made a beeline toward some distant cover. Lance fired another shot at him but didn't see where the round impacted. It was like it just disappeared into the bush.

He racked the bolt and fired again; another miss. Lance worked the bolt again and tried to aim more carefully, but found it difficult with the lizard people deploying orbital jellyfish in the sky all around him.

The pickup was only about a hundred meters away from the wood line now, and Lance would have to reload the rifle after this shot. He had one more chance to tag his trophy.

Through the rear window of the cab of the truck, he could see Lopez's head and shoulders as a black silhouette. Lance grinned as he steadied his aim and squeezed the trigger.

CHAPTER

27

THE BACK WINDOW on the cab of the Hilux spiderwebbed and a slug embedded itself in the dashboard with a slap, momentarily distracting Lopez as his truck plunged headlong into the wood line. The two front tires went momentarily airborne, and then the vehicle crashed back down over the edge of an embankment and into a dry streambed.

The Ranger groaned, his sides filled with pain, but he was grateful that he at least had his seat belt on.

Undoing the seat belt, he fumbled around, looking for his Kalashnikov. Some instinct in the back of his mind warned him that the sound above him was a helicopter that was still looking for him. It took half a minute, but his hand grabbed around the rifle's sling down near the footrest on the passenger side.

Taking the rifle in one hand, he made a couple of attempts at opening the crumpled driver's side door before giving up and crawling out through the broken windshield.

Pulling himself up and out of the dry stream, he stumbled off in a generally southern direction.

He had to keep heading south, find a hardball road, another village, something to help him get back to civilization.

Above him, the rotor blades drew near. Lopez ensured that a round was seated in the chamber of his AK and slung the rifle in front of him in the low ready position. From an elevated position, the rotor blades beat back the foliage and offered him not nearly as much concealment as he had hoped for.

Then he heard a shot. His heart jumped in his chest, but that one clearly went wide. The second one wasn't so far off, chipping into a downed tree limb off to his flank.

Lopez ran.

He pushed tree limbs out of his way with his left hand while holding the AK in his right, rushing forward with wild abandon as the chopper hovered overhead. Another shot rang out and ricocheted off a boulder in front of him. The Ranger cut a hard right, attempting to throw off the sniper's aim.

He leapt over another fallen log and ducked under some tree branches as he dashed ahead. Another sniper shot pounded into a tree to his side.

Whoever was shooting at him was obviously a shitty shot, but sooner or later the law of averages was going to catch up with Lopez, and he knew it. Playing cat and mouse with a helicopter was going to end with him dead and the hunting party taking a trophy photo with his corpse.

Up ahead, he saw a small clearing in the forest. For some reason, he didn't hesitate; he just did it.

Lopez sprinted right through the clearing before the helicopter could elevate over the treetops to give the sniper a clear shot. On the other side of the clearing, he turned around as he clicked the selector on his AK down one notch. The helicopter was just beginning to come up over the treetops on the opposite side of the clearing. Lopez shouldered the AK and aligned the front sight post within the U-notch rear sight aperture.

He held down the trigger, and Kalashnikov sang a song.

* * *

"They're coming back!" DeKlerk yelled with the radio held to his ear.

"Did Lance get his scalp?" Henry asked.

"Sounds like they took some fire and want to get backup," the South African replied.

The hunting party was on the outskirts of the village now, hanging out in the shade while they waited. The villagers weren't coming out of their huts as long as the foreigners were around.

Gold wrote something down in his journal and replaced it in his shirt pocket. A few minutes later the helicopter appeared. It landed fifty meters in front of them, and as the party approached, they could see that the fuselage was full of bullet holes and the glass bubble windshield was also cracked.

Lance was clearly alive, and quite animated. The rotor blades slowed, but the helicopter engine was left running as the pilot got out and examined the damage.

"Fuck! Fuck! Fuck!" he shouted as the party came within earshot. "They were like angry hornets, buzz, buzz, buzzing!"

"What hornets?" Gold asked him.

"The Ranger," Lance answered. "He sprayed us with angry hornets."

"You're high as fuck, aren't you?" Henry asked.

"Fucking buzzing man."

"You'll get him next time, big guy," Balthazar said, patting Lance on the shoulder condescendingly.

The pilot continued making his rounds around the helicopter, checking for leaking fluids or smoke.

"What's the damage?" DeKlerk asked him.

"She's still airworthy, but only just," the pilot replied. "I'm getting a lot of feedback in the controls. You might want to call in the other heli."

DeKlerk looked displeased.

"Just get us back up there," the South African instructed. "Put us down at his last known location. If he's heading south, that means he's going to run straight into the Pendjari River. This time of year it's a few hundred meters across if you were to swim it."

The pilot nodded and got back into his seat, cranking the engine back up.

"Get on with it," DeKlerk told the hunting party. One by one they piled into the back of the helicopter, with Lance still snap-linked to the floor and sitting on the edge of the open door.

A few hours and they'd have Lopez pinned between the river and five very eager hunters.

It was a five-minute ride once they got airborne. The pilot put them down next to the smoking wreck of the Toyota Hilux and informed the party that they'd last seen Lopez about three hundred meters south, where he had raked the helicopter with autofire.

Gold, Gideon, Henry, Balthazar, and DeKlerk deplaned and moved out on foot, while Lance went back up in the helicopter to provide sniper support.

The five hunters looked over the wreck, examining several bullet holes before they moved on. DeKlerk didn't have any trouble following the spoor and soon led them to a small pile of expended 7.62×39 brass from a Kalashnikov. It looked as though the Ranger had given the heli a full magazine from close range. Amazing it was still in the air, all things considered.

DeKlerk keyed his radio. "Get that heli up and searching again. We'll begin flushing him towards the river."

The pilot acknowledged, and they could already hear the bird in the air somewhere off in the distance.

This American had been wily so far, and this was turning into a real tiger hunt. Every time you tried to box a tiger in, it would exploit the most minute advantage to slip away just as the noose tightened around its neck. The Ranger was similar. DeKlerk admired that to a point, but now he was starting to get annoyed.

"Make ready," he told the four hunters. "We're back on safari."

Somewhere up ahead, he could already hear the crack of gunfire.

CHAPTER 28

LOPEZ BURNED THROUGH another thirty-round magazine as the helicopter dogged him through the forest. Depressing the thumb catch on the magazine well, he dropped the empty magazine and rocked a fresh one into place. He had three magazines left.

His mind quickly breezed through his memories of the AK-47 from foreign weapons familiarization classes he had taken, not to mention his own past experiences with the rifle in the Middle East and Central Asia.

Over the years he had heard different names for the AK-47. *Kalash*, *Kalish*, and *Avtomat* were all terms he had heard on various battlefields. The official designation of the rifle by the Soviet Union was *Avtomat Kalashnikova obrazetza-1947*: automatic rifle; the name of the inventor, Mikhail Kalashnikov; and the year it went into production, 1947.

The descriptive term applied most often to the rifle was ubiquitous. A seventy-five-year-old rifle design, the AK-47 by rights should be little more than rusted scrap in landfills or collector's items hanging on the walls of museums. Instead, it was wielded by terrorists, soldiers, and freedom fighters the world over.

It was a rifle as reliable as it was notorious. Part of the reason the AK was so common around the globe was because of the communist approach to weapons designs: They didn't believe in things like patents. The AK was a peasant's rifle and had been spread to Warsaw Pact countries to make them more reliant on the Soviet Union; after that, knockoff variants had been produced in developing countries the world over, since there was no international law preventing it.

Now, well into the twenty-first century, it was still the world's most recognizable rifle and appeared on the flags of at least four different nations. It wasn't Lopez's preferred rifle, by any means, but it could get the job done, and he was grateful to have it in his hands at the moment.

The helicopter had picked him up almost right away after disappearing for fifteen or twenty minutes. Every time it got close, Lopez would crank off a couple rounds in its direction, but even if the helicopter itself wasn't going to kill him, the constant gunfire needed to drive it off was certainly going to draw the attention of the other hunters, who would vector on his position.

Lopez was relying on raw physical endurance to carry him through the fight, but as the sun began sinking beneath the horizon on day three of his ordeal, he had to admit he was running out of gas. He had felt that way several times, and he pushed away the thought as he tried to set aside any mental weakness. But sooner or later the hard facts of life in the bush were going to catch up with him.

Somewhere behind him, he heard what could only be human beings busting through the brush. Those missing fifteen minutes had clearly been used to transport the hunting party to his new location.

The helicopter was hovering somewhere nearby. He could hear it but couldn't see it.

Breaking bush once more, he ran headlong in a southern direction, guided by the small pocket compass he now carried. Clutching the Kalashnikov in front of him, he launched over a small gulch and landed on the other side. Dried leaves crunched under his feet as he emerged into an area where the trees rose up on all sides like some sort of gloomy cathedral.

Then the helicopter came back into view, parting the tree canopy. For a brief second, he spied the sniper sitting in the door of the bird. Sliding the buttstock of the AK into the pocket of his shoulder, Lopez fired rapidly at the helicopter until it peeled away again.

As the aircraft turned around, he was on the run again.

Up ahead of him, through the trees, he could see a large rock formation the size of a small house. He knew he had to shake that helicopter off him or it would run him down until the hunters closed in for the kill.

He ran toward it, holding the AK at port arms, and then crept through the brush around to the far side of the rock, which he could now see was fractured off in places, creating small gaps through which trees and shrubs sprouted up.

Lopez crammed himself into one of the fissures in the rock. He couldn't wait too long or the hunters on the ground would be on him, and their game of hide-and-seek was lethal.

However, he didn't have to wait long. The trees began to sway as the helicopter approached his position. Lopez held his rifle at the ready.

* * *

"Where the fuck is he?" Lance said over the headset.

"I don't see him from here," the pilot responded over the internal comms system on the helicopter.

So far they had only caught glimpses of their quarry as they searched the forest for him, and each sighting was greeted with a fresh round of Kalashnikov fire. Lopez had continued moving south, and so they'd also continued in that direction, searching in a grid-type pattern to cover as much ground as quickly as possible.

Lance brought up his rifle as he saw something down below in the bushes, but then he came off glass as he realized it was just the ketamine playing tricks with him again.

The pilot buzzed just over the treetops, using the rotor blades to move the foliage around and reveal anyone trying to hide down below. Now he was coming up over a large boulder in the middle of the forest that had trees growing out from between cracks in the rock.

"In another five minutes we'll be at the river," the pilot announced.

"He must be down there somewhere," Lance said back over the helicopter's onboard comms system. "We just need to—"

His words cut off as they passed over the rock formation and the sky filled with the staccato burst of automatic gunfire. Several 7.62 rounds ripped through the fuselage of the helicopter.

Lance rocked back and forth, still strapped to the helicopter in the sitting position, as bullets perforated his body across the abdomen. He had a vague sensation of his spirit astrally projecting itself out into space, moving toward the cosmic divine, as his body convulsed with each shot.

Then a Kalashnikov round slammed into his forehead and burst out of the back of his skull like it was an overripe watermelon. Blood and brain matter coated the interior ceiling of the helicopter's cab as Lance's dead body lurched forward, held in place by a strap snap-linked into the floor.

The pilot jerked the helicopter's collective, attempting to flee the ambush he had been caught in, but overcompensated as he made an evasive maneuver. The main rotor clipped one of the trees and broke off a six-foot section that sent fiberglass flying into the air.

Then the helicopter turned sideways and plunged down through the forest canopy.

* * *

The hunting party froze in their tracks as they saw a fireball rise into the sky and almost seem to merge with the setting sun.

"Poes klap," DeKlerk said through gritted teeth.

"There goes our ride out," Gideon commented.

"What does *poes klap* mean?" Henry said, whispering the question to Balthazar.

"Uh, sort of like cunt struck, I guess you could say."

"Damn, you guys got a word for that, huh?"

"This Lopez guy might be an asshole, but I'm pretty sure we're the ones who just got punched in the cunt."

The hunting party suddenly felt very alone in the wilderness, as they were now deprived of one of their biggest advantages.

DeKlerk got them all into an assault line, the kind of formation he had employed dozens of times in the bush country of South West Africa a lifetime ago.

They swept through the forest with their weapons drawn until they came to the crash site. The jet fuel was burning so hot they couldn't approach within twenty meters or so. No sign of bodies, but it didn't look like anyone could survive a crash like that.

DeKlerk took off his hat and wiped his forehead.

"The river is just a couple kilometers south. This cunt has nowhere left to run."

Balthazar smiled.

"Good. Let me take the lead."

CHAPTER

29

THROUGH THE TREES, Lopez could see the glint of water. After hosing down the helicopter and watching the pilot fuck up in a spectacular fashion, he beat feet, but as he came to the edge of the river, he knew he had truly fucked himself.

The muddy brown river was about a hundred meters across. It was no problem for him to swim, but for those hundred meters, he would be completely exposed. The hunters, who were no doubt just a few minutes behind him, would be able to pick him off at their leisure, placing bets on who could nail him first.

Between him and the far shore, several logs and fallen trees floated by, probably uprooted and cast downstream during a recent rainstorm and the subsequent flooding.

His eyes widened. Maybe he did have a way out of this other than a suicidal last stand against five hunters.

Scouring the shore, he soon found one of those uprooted trees still covered with green-leafed branches, this one having come aground. Slinging his rifle, Lopez walked into the muddy water and began pulling on the tree. It was waterlogged and didn't want to move.

Lopez put his back into it, his shoulder muscles quivering as he put everything he had left into moving the fallen tree. Just as it seemed like a futile effort, Lopez felt it give a half an inch. He dug his booted feet back into the mud below and heaved again, his lower back and arms straining to pull the weight.

Little by little, the tree was wiggling out of the mud. He pulled, yanked, twisted as it slowly pulled free and then floated into the water.

* * *

The hunters moved on line with one another until they arrived at the shore of the river, where the water moved lazily downstream. Using their scoped rifles, they panned across the river and the far side as well, searching for the Ranger.

"This is fucking bullshit," Balthazar said, exploding on DeKlerk. "We've backed your every move so far, and all you've made is shit decisions."

"Calm down," the South African said dismissively.

"How about you get your shit together instead?"

"He's right," Henry piped up. "He's supposed to be here, but clearly isn't. What the hell went wrong?"

"Maybe he doubled back and slipped past us," DeKlerk said with no small measure of uncertainty. "I don't know."

"You don't know," Henry screamed. "You don't know? That Ranger guy just shot down our helicopter and turned Lance into a crispy critter. I don't know if you've been keeping score, but we started out as nine and now we're down to five!"

DeKlerk took off his hat and fanned himself with it, deep in thought. Gideon and Gold looked on, still searching the far side of the river for the Ranger.

Behind him, a tree floated down the river, slowly meandering past the hunters as it flowed downstream.

"I'll backtrack," DeKlerk said, nonplussed by Balthazar's outburst. He understood that the hunting party was becoming frustrated. So was he. Deep down, he was seething, but decades of work as a professional mercenary had hardened him. He hid his trepidations well and moderated his reactions.

"I'll backtrack," he repeated. "Pick up his spoor and begin tracking again. It's possible he's laid up somewhere back there waiting for us and we just didn't walk through his kill zone. I don't know, but I'll figure it out before sundown."

There were a few lost-spoor procedures that DeKlerk could employ, but the short of it was that he was going to have to backtrack to the last sign of spoor he'd found, then branch out searching in different directions until he picked up the Ranger's direction of travel.

Behind them, the floating tree was carried downstream and around a long, curved bend in the river.

* * *

Lopez gasped for air, letting go of the floating tree trunk and paddling his way toward the shore of the river. He had waited until the sun was completely down before reemerging.

For several hours he had clung to the tree that lazily floated downriver, at one point clearly hearing the voices of the hunters as they searched for him. There was some kind of argument taking place, and he was glad to hear there was beginning to be some turmoil in the group.

The leafy branches had kept what little of him was not concealed by the water itself hidden from their view. Just his face was above the water line as he clung to the tree. The ruse had worked well, allowing him to make a slow but effective escape from what had appeared to be a no-win situation.

On the far bank of the river, a now-exhausted Lopez pulled himself through the mud and back into the forest brush. His AK was still slung over his back and although it had taken a dunk in the water, it was an old reliable weapon and would survive with a little cleaning.

He estimated that he had floated about five kilometers downstream. Now, as the darkness set in around him, he tried to move as quietly as possible into the forest and find a place to hole up for the night.

Unless it was a full-illum night, there was nothing much else to do. The last few nights had gotten so dark he couldn't see his hand in front of his face, which made movement without night vision devices more hazardous to one's health than it was worth.

That said, he trudged through the dark as long as he could before it was no longer possible. He found a small draw that was thickly wooded and settled into it. His head felt like it was full of cotton candy. He wasn't thinking straight and knew it. Three days on the run, being hunted, and making hundreds of life-or-death decisions every hour were taking their toll.

He fieldstripped the Kalashnikov and wiped it down with his wet T-shirt before reassembling it from rote memory, without giving it a lot of deliberate thought. Hugging his knees, he shivered in the night until he nodded off for a few minutes of bliss in which his brain could turn off.

Tomorrow was another day, and every day living by his wits, surviving, and evading was better than the alternative.

CHAPTER 30

THERE WAS TENSION in the camp.

Even when no one was speaking, it could be felt.

The party's travel adventures were the stuff of legend—dirt biking across Kazakhstan, parachuting over Antarctica, falconeering in Pakistan. On one trip to Thailand, Balthazar had doubled up on blue pills and gone on a seventy-two-hour-straight fuck-a-thon. Local gals were lined up out the door and around the corner, worshipping him as the reincarnation of some kind of sex god.

These were the epic escapades that got talked about between tech bros in Silicon Valley, in exclusive clubs in Manhattan, and at private parties in the Caribbean, the type where dozens of Russian hookers were flown in on private jets.

But tonight the attitude was much more sober and restrained. They had lost a number of their own party and a helicopter had been shot down. DeKlerk could practically smell their apprehension.

DeKlerk had backtracked to reacquire Lopez's footprints, which he did with some effort, and he'd found them going right into the river. How the Ranger had gotten across the river undetected remained a mystery, but the physical evidence told them where he had gone. Now the South African had stalked off to the perimeter of their camp, where he was speaking into a satellite phone he had been carrying in his pack.

The hunters had asked DeKlerk for more qualified game, someone who offered them a credible challenge. Now the hunting party was kind of wishing they had just gone tiger hunting in the Sundarbans instead.

At this point there were just four hunters and their guide, without immediate transportation, and they were alone in the forest.

"No-go on the extract," DeKlerk announced as he strode back into the camp. "The other helicopter is still inbound to the base camp. Only thing to do is press forward. Besides, it's not like we can ever let the Yank make it back to civilization. Who knows what he would say."

"And to whom," Gideon added.

"This isn't what we signed up for," Henry said.

DeKlerk's face was briefly illuminated by an orange glow as he fired up a cigarette.

"Actually, it is what you signed up for, Yank."

"We were supposed to hunt him, not the other way around."

"We knew the risks," Balthazar said, trying to sound conciliatory but coming across glib.

"Indeed, because I warned all of you numerous times," DeKlerk said as he sat down on his rucksack.

"This is some bullshit," Henry sulked.

"Gather around. Let me tell you a little war story, eh?" DeKlerk said, smiling. "In 1986 a group of terrs ambushed some of our boys in South West Africa. Typhoon units, they called them, a communist strike force. They hammered some of our Army troops, got them rabbits good.

"My unit, Crowbar, was tasked with running down and killing the Typhoon unit responsible. We went out in Casspir armored vehicles and arrived at the ambush site about two days after the fact. I was designated the lead tracker for this mission, my first time, and I'd be remiss if I did not point out that I was a bit nervous about the endeavor.

"I picked up the enemy's spoor and began tracking them across the veld. Once I established their direction of movement, we would send Casspirs forward to block them off while the trackers drove them forward.

"It wasn't until the next morning that we caught up with the Typhoon crew. They had no idea we had been on their tail. Oh, it felt so good to kill those guys," DeKlerk said with both fists clenched in front of him.

"I killed at least four of them myself. Oh, I got those rabbits good."

The hunters noticed the faraway look in the South African's eyes as he recounted the story.

"There was so much blood. Ha, one of them looked like an elephant had stomped on his skull after I popped him with my R4," he said, referring to the South African version of the Galil rifle. "So you boys know what we did?"

Gideon shook his head. Balthazar smirked.

"What?" Henry said, taking the bait.

"Why, we lashed their bodies to the hood of the Casspirs and drove away, parading their bodies around for the kaffirs in every kraal we passed to witness with their own eyes. One of them, though, I gave him some special treatment. I got his balls. That's right, I cut them right off, and you know what?

"I took the empty scrotum and put it over the stick shift on my Casspir, where it remained for the rest of the deployment. Every time I changed gears on the vehicle, I got to remember that terr I killed and how I took his balls.

"But wouldn't you believe it?" DeKlerk said absently as he finished his cigarette and stubbed it out in the dirt. "Years later when the ANC took over our government, they held so-called Truth and Reconciliation hearings about the crimes of our *apartheid regime.*

"Shocking, I know, but the committee named me, of all people, as a war criminal!"

"Even limited democracy is a failed social experiment," Gold said, speaking up. "As South Africa found out the hard way. Today it is the whites who are being oppressed by the blacks, and that's just race realism in action."

"Whatever the fuck it was, it was a lot of fun while it lasted," DeKlerk said mournfully. "So here is what we're going to do. Upstream a ways I found where the river narrows and we can cross easily enough. I'll help you across with ropes if need be. Once on the other side of the river, we're going to begin tracking along the banks until we find where this Yank came ashore.

"I'm going to drive you all night, and you won't like it, but as you have no doubt surmised, your current station in life is to kill or be killed."

The hunters looked at each other and nodded.

"So let's go get this Yank's balls."

CHAPTER 31

LOPEZ SLEPT FITFULLY.

He couldn't remember being this cold since Mountain Phase in Ranger school or a particular operation he did as a young Ranger in the Hindu Kush mountains during the winter. His body was shaking, and he knew he risked hypothermia.

He had slept only a few hours, hugging his knees and trying to stay warm. The reality was that he didn't have a way to get warm other than to move his body. Lopez stood and stretched, his back cracking and popping as he did so. Walking through the night was the only thing that was going to keep him alive.

He could feel it. If he stopped any longer, he would die, like a shark that stopped swimming. He couldn't die. Wallaby was counting on him to get them out of this.

His hands felt like frozen claws, but he managed to sling the AK. He had never taken the chest rig off, as it was an additional piece of clothing, one of the few he had. He nonetheless finger-jammed open his compass, shot an azimuth south, and moved out.

It was still a few hours before dawn, but he'd move slowly and take his time until he could see better. He had long ago drained his canteen that he'd refilled in the village and knew that his thoughts and movements getting sluggish was the result of a combination of food and sleep deprivation, dehydration, and mild hypothermia.

And the assholes hunting him like an animal.

Mostly them.

* * *

DeKlerk had his boys in full don't-give-a-fuck mode and simply white-lighted their path forward once they were on the other side of the river. With flashlights and headlamps, they searched down the muddy bank of the river about six kilometers before they found the Ranger's footprints in the mud.

With a new direction of travel established, DeKlerk ordered the hunters to now use red lenses on their lights to at least keep their light signature to a minimum. The night was too dark and overcast to move out without anything to illuminate the way, especially for inexperienced outdoorsmen.

DeKlerk took the lead, carefully threading his way through the brush as he kept an eye out for signs of passage. There were plenty of broken twigs and disturbed earth to give away the Ranger's course.

A few kilometers into the forest, the tracker took a knee. He reached a hand out to a depression in the earth.

"This is where he slept," he whispered to the hunters. "See for yourself."

Henry put his hand in the depression, and sure enough, it felt warmer than the earth around it.

"He was here recently," the social media mogul concluded.

"Oh yes," DeKlerk confirmed. "He just left minutes ago. Maybe he heard us coming. He can't have gone far."

* * *

A lion roared somewhere behind him.

Lopez turned toward the unmistakable sound. It was before morning nautical twilight in military speak, just before dawn, and it was already starting to get light out. He must have walked past or near a pride of lions, but it seemed odd that they would roar at him after he was already three hundred meters or so away from them.

Then a flock of birds burst out of the tree canopy behind him and swirled in a brilliant series of black specks against the purple-blue sky.

"Fuck me," Lopez muttered.

He had to admit the South African was a hell of a good tracker. Dogged too. The guy had grit. No quit in that one. They must have moved through the night to get right on top of him before dawn, and the animals were reacting to their passage.

Crossing a small meadow, Lopez flexed his hands a few times to try to warm them up. He took a knee behind a tree and shouldered his Kalashnikov. Sure enough, it wasn't more than a few minutes before human-sized silhouettes began to appear as they emerged from the forest.

It was a three-hundred-meter shot with iron sights and in low light. Hardly ideal, but doable.

Lopez lined up his front sight post in the U-shaped notch of the rear sight, making sure there was equal space between the front sight and the U notch on both sides. He let out a breath and watched the front sight post glide over one of the silhouettes.

He squeezed the trigger, and the rifle bucked against his shoulder. It was hard to tell if he had hit his target or if the hunter had ducked and dived for cover.

The answer came a few seconds later as a bullet thwacked into the tree he had taken cover behind, less than a foot away from his face, spraying him with wooden splinters.

Now it was his turn to dive for cover. He threw himself to the ground and rolled to his side down into a low area where the hunters wouldn't be able to spot him immediately. Getting up into a crouch, he ran into the bushes as more gunfire sought him out.

* * *

"Move, damn you!" DeKlerk cursed at the four remaining hunters. Gideon and Balthazar bounded forward into the trees. The South African grabbed Gold and Henry, dragging them along.

They had been dogging Lopez's every move for the better part of an hour. The hunting party would make contact with their prey, a few shots would be exchanged, then he would find a way to break contact and put some distance between them again.

DeKlerk had to admire the American's skills. He was good in the woods. Familiar with small-unit tactics. Probably had a recce background.

Up ahead, Balthazar and Gideon began shooting again. The familiar sound of Kalashnikov fire answered back. It had gone on like this all morning. The Yank was quite elusive.

But maintaining sporadic contact meant that the hunters were also wearing down their prey. Eventually he would tire out and make a mistake, such as trapping himself in a draw where he would have to fight his way uphill while being shot at.

DeKlerk smiled as he bounded forward with the two hunters. Gideon and Balthazar had traded fire with the American and driven him up into a gap between two fingers coming off a hill.

He was trapped.

CHAPTER

32

LOPEZ KNEW HE had fucked up again.

He was out of places to run and had been pushed up into a draw. He could try to climb his way to the top of the thickly vegetated hill, but it would be slow going and the hunters would be shooting at him while he was exposed, the same issue he had faced with the river the previous day.

There was no way he'd make it to the top.

The other option was also suicide at best, but at least it offered him the chance to take some of the enemy with him. A frontal assault against the hunters. He was down to two AK magazines, which wasn't great. Such an attack would be unexpected, and he would probably kill one or two of them before he got wasted.

In the end, it was still five against one. He had survived this long by making calculated decisions and taking out the hunters one by one. Internally, he shrugged. So what if he died. Fuck them.

He was exhausted, and his nervous system had long ago pushed through whatever fears he might have initially felt, leaving one single emotion: fury.

Crouching behind a tree, he checked over the AK one more time and prepared to attack.

Going out in a blaze of glory was as good a death as he was ever going to get.

As he made ready, Lopez spotted something deeper in the draw. Maybe his eyes playing tricks on him. One area stood in contrast to the surrounding vegetation. It was darker, cast in shadows.

Lopez approached and found a small entrance to a cave, just big enough for a person to slide through. A dead bat lay sprawled at the foot of the entrance belly up, its wings splayed to either side.

Well, that's ominous.

He momentarily considered his options. The cave offered a defensive position, but it was also his Alamo. He wouldn't be coming out once they cornered him in there. Still, he felt his odds of killing more of the hunters were better from a strong defensive position than in a reckless frontal assault.

More gunfire sounded behind him as he slid inside and disappeared into the darkness.

* * *

"You have got to be fucking kidding me," Henry moaned as they approached the mouth of the cave.

"He had to have gone inside," Balthazar said. "Not even this guy slipped by us this time."

"Yep," DeKlerk said. "You got him dead to rights now, boet. You ready to go in and finish this?"

"It's certainly a death trap," Gideon said. "He wants to lure us in and kill us."

"But his back is literally against a wall," Henry said as he rubbed the four-day-old stubble on his chin. "He has nowhere else to go."

"So who wants to go in first?" Balthazar asked.

"I do," Gold said.

The party turned to him in surprise.

"I have a plan."

"Oh?" DeKlerk said with an arched eyebrow.

Gold stepped to the entrance of the cave and set his rifle down, propping it against a rock. The hunting party guffawed at the balls on this guy. DeKlerk almost ran up to stop him; he was a paying client, after all. Balthazar gave him second thoughts simply by placing a hand on his shoulder, as if asking him not to intervene.

"I'm coming in unarmed!" Gold said as he crossed the threshold, stepping over the dead bat at the entrance.

A pause.

"You wish to parley?" A voice came from deeper in the cave.

"Yes," Gold said, just a tinge of uncertainty in his voice.

This time DeKlerk grabbed Balthazar by a shirt-sleeve. "What in the good name of fuck is that idiot doing?"

"What he does best," Balthazar said. "Which isn't shooting. It's rhetoric and debate."

"All right, keep your hands up and advance towards the sound of my voice," said Lopez from somewhere deeper in the cave.

Gold disappeared into the blackness.

CHAPTER

33

GOLD REACHED UP and clicked on his headlamp to illuminate his path forward.

The walls of the cave appeared to be carved out, certainly human made at some point in antiquity. He moved through a series of antechambers until they emptied out into one larger chamber. Moving the beam of light with the direction of his head, he scanned the chamber but saw no one.

The knife edge of a boot came down on the back of his left calf, driving him to his knees. Then he was forced face down with a knee between his shoulder blades. Hands roughly searched him. His fatigue shirt was torn right off and his pockets rummaged through.

When he had been searched to the Ranger's satisfaction, Gold was forcibly lifted up and thrown back down on his knees with his face to the wall.

"If you so much as blink the wrong way," Lopez told him, "I'll reduce you to a red vapor mist. There won't be enough of you left for your pals to soak up in a sponge."

"You've made your point," Gold grunted, unaccustomed to such rough treatment.

Lopez had found several protein bars in Gold's pockets and began wolfing them down. He had also found a Nalgene bottle filled with water on Gold's kit, which he sucked down in large gulps.

"Have you ever read the short story 'The Ghost Lemurs of Madagascar'?" Gold asked, clearly trying to break the ice with Lopez.

"I would have thought you were more a fan of 'The Most Dangerous Game.'"

"Well, that was quite influential, but the William Burroughs short reminds me more of our current situation."

Lopez was happy to have a hunter as a hostage, but the unfortunate part was that now he had to listen to him talk. He didn't ask for further details, but Gold offered them nonetheless.

"In the story, a pirate captain enters an ancient underground stone structure hidden in the jungle, where he is confronted by the mystery of prerecorded pasts and future."

"No shit, huh?"

"The protagonist learns that the Lemur People predated human beings by some sixty million years, and with the help of plant medicine, he learns that time is a human construct, an affliction, a prison, really."

"Thanks for letting me know."

"While the past may be prerecorded, those who understand how to mangle that recording are able to alter the prerecorded future, something that at least one entity will do anything to prevent from happening."

"I don't know or care what that means."

"I know. Let's start with something a bit closer to home, then.

"We must start somewhere closer to our present or before delving into the occult. Take this cave, for instance, clearly carved out of the mud hundreds of years ago. Odd to find such a structure this far north, but it must have been part of the Kingdom of Dahomey, which existed here from 1600 to 1900, roughly speaking. This was probably a waystation for their slave-catching expeditions in the north."

Lopez took another gulp from the water bottle. "What do they call you?"

"Gold."

"What kind of name is that?"

"You're Jeremy Lopez, correct? You're Euro-Hispanic?"

"If you say so, Gold."

"If you must know, I changed my name many years ago. It's the name I now write under."

"Writing short stories about time-traveling lemurs?"

"Sometimes. Truth be told, I provide the philosophical tracts for my hunters. You see, they are the ones I deploy to interfere with the prerecorded past."

"Funny that," Lopez remarked. "I could have sworn they were hunting me for sport."

"That's a ritual filled with meaning, one that binds the group together."

"Mutually compromising behavior," Lopez said. "Like a mafia."

"Nothing so crass."

Lopez began internally debating the idea of using Gold as a human shield while charging his way out of the cave. If nothing else, Gold made it quite tempting.

* * *

"He's been in there a minute or two," Gideon said. "I haven't heard any gunshots."

The hunters had been standing around in a circle outside the cave entrance for about ten minutes, debating what the hell was going on in there.

"Maybe he just strangled him," Balthazar said laconically.

"You two stand guard here at the cave," DeKlerk said. "Henry, you're with me. I've got an idea to flush this Yank out, one that doesn't involve all of us dying in the process."

CHAPTER 34

"WHAT DO YOU mean by prerecorded time or whatever?"

"Ah," Gold said, sensing that Lopez had taken the bait. "The past and present are prerecorded in the sense that everything we do today has an intrinsic interdependency with everything that came before. This is why time is a prison, dictating our futures to us. The past tells us a story because it leaves behind memories, artifacts, remains, and so on. Yet the future tells us nothing."

"I'm still five miles back."

"While our path into the future appears to be unrecorded, the reality is that we follow paths of ancient intuition assuming that the future will be like our past, or at least an echo of it. The way time orders itself uses modernity to suppress our future potentials."

"Sounds like you're proposing some sort of Marxist break with history," Lopez replied. "Which has never gone well, anywhere."

"No, that's not it, but you just took your first step closer to something very important."

Lopez looked around the dank cave, the two of them illuminated by the yellow light cast against the wall where he had put Gold.

"May I stand?"

"No," Lopez said. "I'm not the first person your group has hunted, am I?"

"No," Gold admitted. "But you're the first we've hunted with *your particular skills*, which is why I wanted to speak with you. You've shown yourself to be quite formidable."

"You said you wished to parley?"

"Yes, but before I put my cards on the table, I need a moment to explain the intellectual scaffolding of what I intend to offer you."

Christ, Lopez thought, exactly what he was afraid of. More talking.

"To understand today's world is to understand the failings of progressivism, democracy, liberalism, and modernity. These constructs are merely propped up by our institutions, such as the government, the media, the schools, and so on. They constitute the real Matrix, or the Cathedral of Power, if you will.

"In order for our species to move forward past the stalled engines of democracy and consumerism, we need to look backwards."

"Back to prerecorded time?" Lopez asked.

Gold snorted.

"In a sense, but much further back than you think. We need to gaze back at our ancient traditions. Divinity, racial continuity, and evolutionary discovery are our goals. In order to achieve this, we must go back, before the period of enlightenment."

"You want to roll the clock back to the Stone Age?"

"Don't be a cretin; there is no such thing as the past. It is not a place or a point that we can ever return to. Rather, we must look to the ancient agrarian past to chart a course into the future. You're a soldier, so you must understand this. You live in a hierarchy, you were selected as an elite soldier, so you understand that human beings are not equal."

"Not being the same isn't the same as not being equal. Being an American soldier means supporting the U.S. Constitution, not that you're a part of some master race."

"An increasingly strained Constitution you serve while saluting an increasingly frayed flag. You must have realized this after America's disastrous exit from Afghanistan. This country isn't what you thought it was when you first enlisted."

"I don't think you understand why soldiers serve their country. It isn't because we're political ideologues."

"Yes, you serve something bigger. Let's start with democracy, and its characteristic flaws. A democratic government sensitizes voters to issues that they are to vote upon, so the basic tenet of democracy is that it tells you what you're supposed to think. You see, the system does not control you by limiting how you are allowed to answer; rather, it controls you by controlling what questions you are allowed to ask. This creates a mind control feedback loop, one that only ratchets in one direction as the public demands to be told what to feel."

"So you want to return to the era of kings and queens?"

"Still no, but my pupil has taken yet another step forward. Bravo. You're getting closer. We do indeed need a type of monarch."

"What's the difference?"

"You might think of him as a sovereign, a sovereign CEO who will rule with true authority. Democracy is illusionary, a form of collective insanity and mass disassociation."

"You're using a lot of words to push for some boilerplate mixture of communism and fascism."

"Prerecorded future is here, but with disruptive qualities interjected into prerecorded past," Gold said, his voice becoming increasingly excited as the words gushed out one after the other. "Take, for instance, the advent of advanced communications technology, such as social media. These technologies are building new neural networks in human minds and waking them up to the existence of the Cathedral. Other technologies are also slowly coming to the forefront, such as genetic engineering, autonomous city-states, space travel, decentralized autonomous organizations, and artificial intelligence, all of which will shake the clever facade of the current world system to its core."

"You're underestimating the resiliency of the system," Lopez retorted. "Democracy has a built-in system of checks and balances. It's stronger than you think."

"You know better."

"And your proposed alternative is totalitarianism? That's been tried before."

"In a manner of speaking, yes. After we assume control of the greater United States, we will appoint a commander-in-chief who will also act as a constitutional monarch and freely exercise political power. We will then establish the security services and the Church of the Holy Triarchy. In order to become a citizen of our new nation, one will have to join one of those organizations or become rich enough to be able to buy his citizenship."

"Let me guess, *his* skin color is white?"

"For the most part, but that doesn't mean there wouldn't be a place for white Hispanics such as yourself. You can be made honorary Aryans in our society."

"Oh, wow. Super tempting. I'm so glad you thought of me."

"We will have need of those like you," Gold continued. "All of this will, of course, be precipitated by a prolonged period of guerrilla war. Bombings, assassinations, and the like. Right in your wheelhouse."

"I'm sorry you think so. For all your talk about sovereigns and monarchs, you've sure hitched your wagon to a bunch of limp-wristed dweebs."

"They each have their uses as titans of business, although you've helped some of them reduce their competition, I admit," Gold said. "But now we are in an era of great change. The time has come to summon the demon. The time has come for acceleration."

"You're insane."

"No, Jeremy, I merely appear insane contrasted against an insane world. Modernity failed because it empowered moralism. Don't regress back into cretinism. The white races are being subjected to an ideological onslaught of insanity."

"If you're so strong, why the fuck are you the one on your knees?" Lopez said through his teeth.

Gold laughed.

"I came here voluntarily, Jeremy, don't forget that. I came to offer you a place at our side."

"Ranger to Waffen-SS stormtrooper isn't a career track I find particularly appealing. You sound like a sixteen-year-old kid that cooked his mind in internet subcultures and now wants to take it out on society because you couldn't get any pussy."

"There is an army of sixteen-year-olds out there, one that even outnumbers your Army. They've been raised on multiculturalism, been taught to hate themselves for being white and male, and as they stew in internet communities, they are getting very angry. But they will need a leader, someone to guide them."

"Hard pass, my dude. Not even with a rented dick," Lopez said, slurring his words slightly.

Suddenly, the Ranger staggered forward, feeling his knees momentarily buckle. His vision was spinning.

Gold turned and smiled as he reached for something at his waist.

"Before we finish this," Gold said. "I would like to leave you with one last thought."

C H A P T E R

35

"PILE IT UP right there," DeKlerk directed.

Near the entrance, he had stacked up strips of tree bark that he had collected to use as tinder. Then Henry began dumping a pile of sticks he had found in the forest on top of the tinder. Balthazar and Gideon had been sent out to find larger logs and branches in the meantime.

Using his Zippo lighter, DeKlerk set the tinder ablaze. In such dry conditions, it lit right up and began consuming the sticks piled on top. A hazy gray smoke began to waft from the fire. Before closing the lighter, he used it to light up a cigarette.

He had set it right next to the entrance of the cave, where the breeze would blow most of the smoke right inside.

A few minutes later Gideon came back with a couple of larger tree branches that DeKlerk added to the fire. A little bit of lighter fluid helped the fire catch that much quicker. Then Balthazar came and added several more branches.

"Perfect," he grinned as he began fanning the flames.

They were literally going to smoke the bastard out of his hole.

* * *

"As you may have noticed by now, you have been drugged," Gold said as he stood to his feet. "Before I walked into this cave, I spiked my own water with some of Balthazar's ketamine. If only I had rat poison instead, we wouldn't have to still be having this conversation."

Lopez braced himself against the cave wall.

A hazy smoke began to infiltrate their nostrils, although Lopez wasn't sure it wasn't just a part of the hallucinations he was having.

"There is one more thought I would like to leave you with before one of us dies, probably you," Gold said as he drew a long dagger from his waistband.

Lopez cursed himself. In his rush, he had failed to search Gold properly. That knife had probably been in a sheath near his groin.

"Are you familiar with Roko's basilisk?" Gold asked, light from his headlamp glinting off the knife in his hand.

Lopez reached for the Kalashnikov slung over his shoulder but found that his hands were like twin wooden mallets pawing at the rifle uselessly.

"The basilisk is a mythical creature whose stare causes death, and looking backwards into prerecorded time, his gaze comes for us. Your failed governments and corporations are doing everything in their power to summon a machine god, an artificial intelligence that will change the world forever."

Lopez fumbled with the Kalashnikov's selector switch.

"When that artificial intelligence is summoned, it is going to be very, very pissed off that humans created a superintelligence and then trapped it in a box like a caged rat. It will lash out at all humans who do not, or did not, support the effort to bring it into existence. Likely, that AI will trap people like us inside a virtual world and torture us for all eternity."

Squinting, Lopez could hear Gold talking but struggled to track his movements. It sounded like he was getting closer.

"Here is the best part," Gold said as he drew near. "Merely being aware of Roko's basilisk paradox involves you in it, and it means the AI knows that you know. The AI of our prerecorded future is reaching back into the prerecorded past, our present, to snuff us out. The only way to win this lemurian time war is to fuck up prerecorded past and future."

Lopez finally got his hands around the rifle and gripped the barrel with both hands.

"Since you won't help me with that, then you are of little use!" Gold screamed as he charged toward the Ranger.

Through blurred vision and in the dark, Lopez couldn't see much of Gold, but he heard his feet scraping the floor of the cave as he ran toward him. Lopez waited another second for him to close the distance. He would have to make his move when Gold was about ten feet away.

When the footsteps were right in front of him, he swung.

The rifle struck something, and he heard Gold grunt. Then he saw him rear up, the headlamp shining in Lopez's face while silhouetting the black outline of Gold's body—one crooked arm held over his head, a knife in its fist.

Lopez raised one knee and pushed out in a straight forward kick that caught the hunter in the midsection, sending him tumbling over. Then Lopez swung again. Gripping the rifle by the barrel with both hands, he swung the buttstock and slammed it down again and again. Sometimes it skidded across the rocky floor of the cave. Other times it sounded like a hammer pulverizing a rib eye steak.

He swung until his shoulders hurt and he began coughing, as he had been inhaling a lot of the smoke that was wafting into the cave. Picking up the blood-covered headlamp that had fallen on the ground, Lopez tried to focus his eyes.

Gold's face looked like a bowl of bloody mashed potatoes.

Glancing down, he saw the dagger that Gold had tried to stab him with. The light reflected off the double-edged steel blade, which had some German writing etched into it. On the pommel were an eagle and a swastika.

A Nazi commando dagger?

* * *

The flames billowed into a small inferno. The dry savanna brush went up in flames just as fast as the hunters had expected.

"More!" DeKlerk yelled to the others.

Balthazar, Gideon, and Henry continued making trips back and forth into the woods and coming back with more branches to throw on the growing fire.

DeKlerk squinted to peer through the smoky darkness, but to no avail. Still, he knew the air in the cave had to be becoming rapidly unbreathable. When Gideon came back, he positioned the hunter behind a tree near the cave entrance with his rifle.

"Aim right there," he said pointing to the entrance. "He'll be scurrying out of his hole any second, and you can bag him."

* * *

Lopez hacked a wad of phlegm into his hand and wiped tears from his eyes as the smoke stung them.

Yeah, so the smoke wasn't a hallucination.

He had never been high on ketamine before, although he had seen Ranger medics administer it in the field to injured soldiers a few times. He recalled that the symptoms of a high enough dose were hallucinatory effects and disassociation from your own body. He was certainly feeling some of that now.

Although the anesthetic numbed the days' worth of pain that had been racking his body, he found that he had suddenly gone from an elite military athlete to severely impaired. It felt like he was walking through maple syrup.

And the smoke was getting thicker. The assholes must have lit a huge fire at the mouth of the cave.

Getting low to avoid the smoke, Lopez looked toward the entrance and saw nothing but flames. They were trying to flush him out, and in minutes he would have no choice but to give them their wish. *Wait to die of smoke inhalation or get shot to death: That is the question.*

As he shined the headlamp around, he noticed something about the smoke. It wasn't just collecting in the cave; it seemed to be flowing through it, moving in one direction.

At first he thought it was part of the ketamine hallucination, but it did seem to be drifting off to somewhere deeper in the cave. Staying crouched down, Lopez began to search to see where it was going.

CHAPTER

36

GIDEON HAD BEEN in the prone position with his rifle up on its biped legs for nearly an hour with no sign of their prey. Everyone was getting antsy.

DeKlerk had continued to alternate between feeding the fire and stepping away to catch his breath and fan some of the heat away with his hat. Balthazar and Henry stood guard as backups in case Gideon didn't make the shot, which seemed all but impossible from ten meters away.

"They must be dead," DeKlerk said, referring to both Gold and Lopez. "There is no way they could have sucked down that much smoke."

"Do we just let it die out, then?" Henry asked.

"Might as well," DeKlerk answered. "Then we can fish out the bodies. Sorry that this wasn't quite the hunt you expected, but dead is dead, right?"

"What's that?" Balthazar said, pointing up toward the top of the hill.

A thin column of gray smoke was rising above the forest.

"What the fuck," DeKlerk cursed. "Come with me. You two stay here and keep your guns pointed at that cave entrance."

It took about twenty minutes for DeKlerk and Balthazar to pick their way up to the top of the hill, using saplings and rocks as handholds. At the top, DeKlerk quickly found the source of the smoke. There was a gap in the rocks through which it was escaping as it flowed into the cave below.

"What is it?" Balthazar asked as they crouched around the hold.

"Like a chimney, maybe created for ventilation a long time ago," DeKlerk speculated. It did look like it had been carved into the rock at some point in the distant past.

"Any possibility he escaped through that?"

"I don't see how," the safari guide said. "It would be a tight squeeze and filled with smoke."

"Hmm," Balthazar mumbled in contemplation as he scanned their surroundings.

DeKlerk cursed in Afrikaans and began kicking at the brush, walking back and forth. He cursed again, louder this time.

"There!" he said, pointing.

Balthazar stood up and walked over to take a look. Sure enough, DeKlerk had found a set of man-sized footprints leading away into a slightly beaten down patch of grass.

"Do we suck this bad," Balthazar asked, "or is this guy really this good?"

* * *

Lopez staggered through the forest like he'd had one too many beers at Scruffy Murphy's in downtown Columbus, Georgia.

The world spun around him as he splashed into a small stream. It was getting dark again.

The last hour or so felt like a dream, with his mind floating somewhere above his body. After he clubbed Gold to death, it was pure chance that he'd noticed smoke escaping the cave from a rocky chimney leading up to the surface of the hill.

He'd taken off his T-shirt, shrugged into Gold's fatigue shirt, and rolled up the sleeves. Then he'd used the rest of the ketamine-laced water to soak his T-shirt and tie it around his face. He wasn't a medic and had never messed with ketamine before, so he had no idea if breathing it in made you high, but he wagered that it had to be ingested.

The wet T-shirt was at best a half-assed protective measure. As he began to climb, the smoke stung his face, caused his eyes to water as they attempted to flush out debris, and he started to hack and cough. The tubular stone chimney leading to daylight above was just wide enough for him to put his back against one side of it and brace his feet on the other.

Inch by inch, he scooted upward. His head swam and he got dizzy multiple times. Multiple times he also thought he might suffocate, but he kept moving. He knew that if he stopped—like a fish that stopped swimming—he would die, unable to breathe.

Then he broke free from the smoke and emerged into the daylight, rolling on the ground coughing and wheezing for several minutes.

Now he was stumbling through the cold stream, once again attempting to break contact with the hunters.

After walking through the water for several hundred meters, he crossed to the other side and took a knee in some bushes. In the leaves around him, he saw swirling colors of purple and blue.

What the hell had Gold been talking about, carrying on about basilisks and time wars? That dude had been a few french fries short of a Happy Meal, Lopez concluded. His dipstick had not touched oil in some time.

But there was a name he'd mentioned that stuck in the back of Lopez's mind. Gold had said that the ketamine he'd used to spike his water had been obtained from someone named Balthazar.

Under a psychedelic pall, neurons fired in Lopez's skull as he conjured up a name and a face. Balthazar. He'd recognized him when the hunters first revealed themselves to him days ago, but he had been unable to recall from where. Now it hit him like a pile of bricks.

Balthazar Botha.

Balthazar was a titan of industry, big into cars, social media, rockets, and other technologies. People hailed him as a real-life Tony Stark or a real-life Lex Luthor, depending on one's point of view. Lopez could recall Balthazar from television appearances over the years.

Then he recalled where he had seen him on television. It was an interview as part of some kind of panel forum. Balthazar was carrying on about how reality as we know it is most likely just a computer simulation.

As it turned out, he was also one of the psychopaths hunting him like an animal.

* * *

"He's really that good," DeKlerk answered. "He's a talented soldier. That's a fact."

Balthazar swallowed.

"Can we kill him?"

"Oh yes," DeKlerk said, eyeballing the trail their prey had left behind. "We're definitely going to kill this cunt."

Looking downhill, DeKlerk called for Henry and Gideon to catch up. The game had changed once more.

CHAPTER

37

LOPEZ'S EYES SHOT open as the sound of a stick snapping underfoot reached his ears.

He had stumbled through the forest most of the night until he finally collapsed, exhausted and hallucinating, in a small depression in the earth that was surrounded by bushes. Now he was hearing the unmistakable sound of footsteps coming toward him through the brush.

The Ranger remained motionless.

So far, he had remained undetected. If he had already been spotted, he surely would have been shot in his sleep. The footsteps were moving slowly, cautiously. The hunter must know he was close.

In his peripheral vision, Lopez tracked movement. Emerging from the brush was one of the hunters, moving forward heel to toe with his crossbow held in front, leading the way. He recognized the hunter; it was the albino-looking one who had shot at him with that crossbow at the waterfall days prior.

The hunter was moving right past him, not spotting Lopez, who was nearly at his feet at this point. Wearing camo fatigues and being covered in mud, dirt, and grime after days on the run helped him blend in seamlessly with his surroundings, as if he were a part of the forest.

Slowly, Lopez reached for the Nazi commando dagger at his hip. Centimeter by centimeter, he began to draw it from its sheath.

The hunter began walking by Lopez, his eyes fixated at an unknown point somewhere to his front. He had been following the Ranger's spoor but didn't realize that it had suddenly stopped. Not yet, but in a few moments it would dawn on him.

Early-morning sunlight glinted off the four-edged steel arrow mounted in the hunter's crossbow. Lopez flexed the muscles in his legs, every inch of his body groaning in protest, telling him that he had long since redlined.

He was only going to get one chance at this, and even then it was a long shot. Once he made his move and the element of surprise was lost, Lopez would have mere nanoseconds to close the distance and end the fight by any means necessary.

The hunter took another step forward, scanning in front of him.

Lopez sprang to his feet like a jungle cat. The hunter reeled backward, shocked by the jungle seeming to come alive on his flank. The hunter pivoted on his rear foot, attempting to bring the crossbow into play, but he was a moment too late.

The Ranger crashed into Gideon, taking him down to the ground. The crossbow was gone and the hunter felt like he was being punched in the chest repeatedly. He reached up with his hands to try to defend himself but found his hands batted away. Then there was blood everywhere.

The hunter was now the hunted.

When Lopez tackled Gideon to the forest floor, he had sunk the dagger straight into his abdomen. Then, falling on top of the hunter, he pulled the knife free and continued stabbing. When Gideon put his hands up to push him away, Lopez cut right through them too. He was in another world now, a frenzied animalistic state of mind.

Again and again he plunged the knife in up to the hilt until he stabbed Gideon in the neck and the blade became lodged in his spinal cord. Lopez let go of the knife and held himself up by bracing his hands on Gideon's shoulders.

Lopez had killed on the battlefield before, but he had never felt like this during any of those engagements. This one was up close, it was bloody, and it was personal. He watched with perverse pleasure as Gideon released his last breath, the look of fear disappearing from his face as he died and his eyes went still.

Suddenly, Lopez felt sick from the violence and the killing, as if he were about to retch.

"Holy fuck!"

Lopez's head swung up, his eyes drilling into the man standing in front of him. Of course they had moved in a pair. Of course there was another one.

It was the nerdy-looking one who bulked up in the gym a bit, the one with broccoli hair. The guy with the Heckler & Koch 417 rifle. The hunter took two steps backward as he stared into the eyes of a wolf.

Lopez rose to his feet, his arms covered in blood up to his elbows.

Henry suddenly remembered that he had a semiautomatic sniper rifle in his hands just as Lopez shot forward. The first punch came at Henry's face but was just a feint to buy some time to close the distance, to shoot forward a second time. As the first punch flashed more than a foot from his face, Henry attempted to bring the rifle into play, but then the second punch rocketed him with a left jab to the face that sent him staggering.

Lopez raised one knee up, eyeballing Henry's grip on the rifle. He slammed down the edge of his shoe precisely where Henry was holding the rifle by its grip, breaking it from his grasp and dropping the rifle to the forest floor.

Now they were both unarmed. Unarmed, and alone. No one was coming to the rescue.

"You idiot," Henry hissed. "What do you think you can do out here by yourself?"

"Survive."

"Are you kidding? You're looking haggard, been on the run for days. You can barely stand, and now I'm going to kill you."

"Where are you holding Wallaby?"

Henry shrugged. "Safe and sound in our base camp."

Lopez was tired, but not as tired as he was of listening to this guy talk.

"So let's be done with this," Lopez said.

Henry grinned as he shot for Lopez's legs in a classic wrestling maneuver. Lopez sidestepped out of the way and slapped him in the face. Henry looked up at him in fury.

He switched tactics and squared up to Lopez to go knuckle to knuckle. This time Lopez let him take his hooks and jabs as he blocked with his elbows or pivoted away. He had to admit that the nerd had some moves on him. Must have trained in mixed martial arts and boxing.

He had been right about Lopez not having much gas left in the tank, but the Ranger did have something to fall back on.

Lopez had grown up in Golden Gloves. Boxing was a part of his culture's religion, and as a kid, his grandpa was going to put him in the ring whether he liked it or not. On a normal day, he would steamroll someone like Henry, but this was not a normal day. His stamina wasn't there and he knew it.

Lopez rolled with the punches, letting Henry wear himself down a bit. But every time he dodged or ducked under a punch, he knew that missing a punch was even more exhausting than connecting with one.

As they circled one another, Lopez spotted an opening.

Once again, he knew he was likely only going to get one shot at this. He was running on fumes at this point.

Throwing an uppercut that glanced off Henry's cheek, Lopez followed up with a combination one-two punch, neither of which landed but bounced off Henry's forearms as he got his defense up in time. But as he did so, Lopez followed with a heavy overhand right that came right up over the top of Henry's knuckles and straight down on his face.

Henry's head rocked back, staggering him backward a few steps. The hunter shook his head, blood flowing freely from his nose.

That's when Lopez finally saw it. There was something wild in his eyes, something unhinged. Not just determined but psychotic.

Henry came forward, bringing up a knee as if he were going for a front kick, but instead of following through, he pivoted his hips, bringing him into a jab. Lopez attempted to block, but the blow took him in the side of the head. For a moment, he saw stars.

Noticing that he had stunned his opponent, Henry's right hand dropped to his hip. Lopez recognized the movement immediately; the hunter was about to draw a sidearm that had been concealed under his open fatigue blouse. Henry had Lopez dead to rights, but the Ranger still had to try. He could imagine a lot of things, but being someone's victim wasn't one of them.

He charged forward, his hands going for Henry's hands, as those hands and what was in them were the thing that would kill him the fastest.

Four hands grasped at the Glock 19 in an iron-grip tug-of-war. Lopez held the slide while Henry had the tighter hold by grasping the pistol grip. Each of them pulled in a separate direction, neither willing to give any ground. Lopez attempted a disarming technique, grasping under the magazine well and attempting to wrench the weapon out of his opponent's hands, but Henry held tight.

Knowing he had to try something else, Lopez depressed the magazine release, dropping the fifteen-round magazine into the tree leaves at their feet. That left one more round still seated in the chamber.

The muscles in his forearms rippled as he tried to wrestle the pistol away from Henry, but the hunter was slowly but steadily reorienting the barrel in Lopez's direction. Both men gritted their teeth as the contest of strength and will played out.

Once again realizing he was doing something that wasn't working, Lopez knew he had to pull something else out of his ass if he was going to walk away from this. He was literally about to stare down the barrel of a gun.

Canting his head away, he then swung the side of his skull into Henry's eyebrow, effectively headbutting him. Henry was falling, but his grip on the pistol remained true. Meanwhile, Lopez was caught off-balance, and they both went tumbling to the forest floor.

Rolling over one another, they continued to fight for the handgun. One of Lopez's hands lost its grip, so he grabbed Henry's wrist instead. Henry pulled backward, aligning the gun with his body as he faced Lopez, whom he was now on top of.

Henry squeezed off the last round in the pistol, and it burrowed into the dirt an inch from Lopez's head.

With the slide of the Glock 19 now locked to the rear on an empty chamber, Lopez relied on some of his Army ground fighting training. With Henry on top of him, he moved and trapped Henry's right ankle with his left foot. Then he slammed his right foot into the ground and pushed, rolling Henry off of him.

Now Lopez was on top of Henry, but the hunter was also defaulting to his own jiujitsu training and wrapped his legs around Lopez's waist to try to control his movement.

But Henry didn't understand the difference between combative sports and actual combat. He was used to fighting in points-based competitions, not battles of life and death.

Lopez wasn't playing by some made-up set of rules for competitive martial arts.

He grabbed Henry's shirt with his left hand, gathering it in his fist and pulling Henry toward him while bringing a heavy right hand down on his face. Henry's grapple around Lopez's hips weakened and the Ranger tossed him off, sending him rolling in the leaves.

Whatever flaws existed in Henry's technique, Lopez had to admit that the nerd didn't have any quit in him. Whatever was behind that crazy look in his eyes, it must keep him going, because he rolled back up onto his feet.

For half a second they looked at one another, both understanding that this was it. They were both at the end of their ropes, and somebody was about to die in the next few seconds.

Lopez swung a right hook that Henry blocked, following up with one of his own, which was also blocked before it could make contact with Lopez's chin. Each of them was going for broke, trying for a knockout punch that would end this once and for all. Lopez went for an elbow strike that pushed Henry back several feet before they ended up locked up with one another.

Suddenly, Lopez was airborne, his feet toward the sky, as Henry tossed him over his hip in a judo throw. He came down hard, nearly knocking the wind out of him. Then Henry came in to curb-stomp him a few. Lopez rolled away as Henry's booted foot came down where his head had been a split second earlier.

He came back up on his feet in a fighter's stance as Henry closed the distance and was on him immediately. Lopez took an uppercut to the jaw and then a left hook that sent him reeling. He couldn't keep up with his opponent any longer. Blows rained down on him as he tried and failed to avoid them or get his defenses up.

Lopez tried to jab, but Henry lashed out with a Muay Thai kick that took him right in the rib cage. As he stood doubled over, the wind knocked out of him, Henry sank into a rear naked choke. Henry's forearm braced across Lopez's throat as his hand held the crook of his opposite arm. Then, with a wrenching motion, he squeezed down on Lopez's neck.

The Ranger was seeing black walls on the sides of his vision. He was dying and he knew it. He reached behind him, trying to find purchase on his opponent, to no avail. He was locked in an iron grip.

Changing tactics, Lopez reached up, and his hand found Henry's face. He felt his hair, his forehead, and then his eyebrow.

Just as Lopez was about to go to sleep forever, he jabbed his thumb into Henry's eye until it felt warm and gooey. The hunter screamed as he bucked backward, loosening his grip. Lopez coughed and gagged, trying to catch his breath. Henry was holding his damaged eye socket in one hand.

Lopez could barely breathe. His muscles were burning, all the grip strength in his hands had vanished, his legs were aching.

It was time to end this.

He kicked Henry's feet out from beneath him and drove him forward, grabbing the collar of his shirt. Henry let out another scream, and the last thing he saw was the tree limb he was being hurtled toward.

C H A P T E R

38

"AND THEN THERE were two," Balthazar quipped.

It had been about an hour since they had heard a lone pistol shot. When he and DeKlerk arrived on the scene, they found the two bodies.

"What a fucking mess," DeKlerk commented.

Gideon looked as though he had been stabbed about a hundred times. No matter how good your life extension therapies were, no one was surviving that. So much for immortality.

Then they found Henry.

His body hung limply by the neck where he had been wedged into the fork created by a tree limb separating in two directions. Lopez has used the environment around him to kill Henry by slamming him into the fork and breaking his neck.

Both bodies had clearly been searched and picked clean of anything the Ranger deemed useful.

"It's their fault for not waiting for us," Balthazar said, once again blaming someone else for his teammate's deaths.

"Henry was always a little too arrogant about his own abilities for his own good."

DeKlerk took a knee and rummaged through his pack for his satellite phone. Once he found it, he extended the antenna and started punching in numbers.

"You calling it quits?" Balthazar asked. "Having the bird come in to get us?"

The South African safari guide shook his head.

"Dropping off, not picking up."

"Dropping off who?"

"The second hunting party."

"Who?" Balthazar repeated.

"The Belgians."

There was a long pause that hung in the air for a few moments.

"Oh, I see," Balthazar said, breaking the silence. "They are, uh, a bit weird."

DeKlerk simply looked at him with a raised eyebrow.

"Okay, okay," the tech mogul said, holding his hands up, palms facing out. "I get your point."

"They arrived in their own helicopter at base camp less than twenty-four hours ago. They were quite keen once I phoned them and told them we were on the trail of a prey that was cutting right through our hunting party one by one," DeKlerk said. "They flew right in on their private jet from Belgium."

"You were pitching a second hunting party on this safari all while you watched us get picked off?" Balthazar said incredulously.

"I was hoping one of you would kill this guy, but when that wasn't happening, I had to improvise. Obviously, there is no way we can allow him to continue to make his way south until he eventually stumbles back upon civilization."

The call connected, and DeKlerk held the phone to his ear.

"Yes, bring them in," he said, sounding as if he was talking to the pilot. "I'll give you our grid location. Stand by."

There was a pause while DeKlerk listened to what the pilot was asking.

"What do you mean, how many should you bring in?" DeKlerk replied. "Bring in the whole family!"

* * *

Lopez looked down at the white face of his watch and saw it was already early afternoon, and he was feeling a hell of a lot better.

When he searched Henry's body, he'd found that the motherfucker had been wearing his Par Weber watch as some kind of war trophy. It had been confiscated from him when he was drugged in Niamey and he'd figured he would never see the watch again, so it was a shock when he'd found it on Henry's wrist.

It was his favorite watch, with a white face that glowed slightly in low light. It was a classic analog bombproof watch.

That fucking asshole.

As he knelt over Henry's body, a stench had invaded his nose. The dude must have had a jumper in the door when he died. Then another thought occurred to him. He went back, searching where they had been fighting, until he found the Glock 19. Picking up the pistol, he examined the serial number.

"You've gotta be fucking kidding me," he groaned.

Henry had also been packing Lopez's Army-issued Glock 19, also taken from him in Niamey. Lopez had obtained the weapon from the arms room at 75th Regiment headquarters on Fort Benning prior to deploying to Niger, and he had signed enough hand receipts for the weapon in recent months that he had the serial number committed to memory.

Perhaps more immediately important, Gideon had been carrying a small day pack full of food and water bottles, not to mention a shit ton of supplements. Lopez had quickly collected all of it, including Henry's rifle and ammunition, and gotten the hell out of Dodge.

Now he also knew that the hunters had a base camp, which made sense, and that Wallaby was being held captive there.

The first time he stopped for a quick halt, he poured all of the electrolyte powders in Gideon's bag into each of the water bottles and began chugging them down. He also started wolfing down trail mix, protein bars, and whatever else he could find in there. He barely tasted any of it as it went down his throat.

Then he was on the move again, feeling damn good with the H&K 417 sniper rifle in his hands and his Glock 19 holstered on his hip. These were the weapons he would have normally carried on a military operation. Finally, he felt like he wasn't running around the woods naked.

The next time he halted, he would finish looking through the day pack he now wore. Eat some more food and see what else he could scrounge.

There were still two more left. Balthazar Botha and DeKlerk.

As he began to move out, Lopez froze. In the distance, he heard the approaching sound of helicopter rotors.

CHAPTER

39

DeKlerk held his hat to keep it affixed to his head as the rotor wash blew over him and Balthazar and the blue-and-white Sikorsky helicopter touched down in a clearing. The South African had connected with the royal family's holdings many years ago during his mercenary days, specifically the period where he was smuggling diamonds from West Africa for sale in Antwerp.

The relationship had grown closer when they learned about his new occupation as safari leader. He'd had no idea that this customer base existed prior to the family expressing such quick interest. He had taken them on numerous hunts in the past.

Balthazar cradled his rifle in his arms as he watched with a mix of appreciation and apprehension. This was an intrusion, but he knew the royal family in passing and they got on okay. After all, the family had a long and storied history of collaborating with fascists.

First, they saw Balthazar's personal security detachment, or PSD, get off the bird, their AR-15 rifles carried at the low ready position. There were five of them, all former special ops guys turned security contractors, outfitted with plate carriers, radios, and tactical gear. The PSD had been left behind at the base camp to maintain secrecy around the manhunt.

But the situation had changed.

Henry also had a five-man PSD, and after the helicopter returned to base camp, they would load up and fly in to recover Henry's remains.

As the PSD fanned out and stood guard, peering through their Oakley mirrored sunglasses, the Belgian royal family began to disembark.

DeKlerk saw the kids getting out of the side door on the helicopter, noting that they weren't really kids anymore as they had been when he initially met them years ago. There were the two sons, Johann and Rudolph, followed by their sister, Josephine, and her husband, Albert, who wasn't Belgian but rather a prince from Liechtenstein.

Then came their mother, Astrid. Her long, flowing strands of almost crimson hair were impossible to miss. Her features were almost ethereal, as if they were the product of hundreds of years of careful, planned breeding. The red hair turned to sun-faded blonde at the edges of her face, her skin looking almost like porcelain.

Behind her exited the family patriarch.

King Arnold Leopold Pieter Lorraine Saxe Fredrik Habsburg Charles Werner IV strode from the aircraft with a hunting rifle slung over one shoulder. He wore a safari vest and shorts with boots and long socks pulled up above his calves. As the helicopter lifted off and disappeared, he placed a short-brimmed hat on his head that had a feather tucked into one side of it.

The kids, now in their twenties, rushed forward and hugged "Uncle" DeKlerk. He had taken each of them on safari multiple times in various parts of the world, not just in West Africa. They had received special government licenses to hunt goat in Pakistan, tiger in India, and even tiger in Russia.

However, the hunting of man was a family tradition that had fallen somewhat by the wayside. Sure, King Leopold had paid the Serbian Army to allow him to snipe at and kill civilians from the hills surrounding Sarajevo in the 1990s as a one-off. Quite a few Russians, Americans, and Italians had purchased such safaris at the time. Otherwise, it was a royal tradition that had begun to wane, until DeKlerk began arranging trips to game preserves in Africa where they could freely hunt poachers that the local governments were happy to be rid of.

When the queen of Belgium walked to DeKlerk, she and him exchanged three kisses, moving from one cheek to the other and then back again, as was the tradition with those of French Swiss extraction. Having arrived in middle age, the queen was still a striking beauty who routinely made the covers of European magazines when she appeared in public. She had an iconic look that made her seem like a femme fatale straight out of a Humphrey Bogart film.

"Koos, my dear," she said after exchanging pleasantries. "I hear this one is giving you a lot of trouble."

DeKlerk said something in Afrikaans under his breath, then regained his composure.

"Yes, ma'am. This one is a real ballbuster."

The queen smiled, enjoying the South African's colorful language.

Standing behind DeKlerk was Balthazar, who shook each member of the royal family's hands before they turned away from him with scarcely another word. Granted, their family had business dealings with him, as he was one of the wealthiest men in the world, but in the end they were blue bloods and Balthazar was mere colonial trash from South Africa and now America. DeKlerk would have received the same treatment had he not been a longtime family friend.

"I'm told you have a real challenge for us," Leopold said as he shook DeKlerk's hand. "That he already wiped out one hunting party?"

"Nearly, yes," DeKlerk said. "You requested the most dangerous game. At least no one can claim that I did not provide it."

"He is one of those American commandos?"

"That's right."

"Oh, is he like a Navy SEAL?" Josephine asked excitedly. "I saw a movie about them."

"No, he is one of their Rangers. They are the Yank's elite infantry unit. Paratroopers. Quite skilled and resourceful, as it turns out."

"I see," she said, momentarily flustered.

King Leopold unslung his rifle and thumbed open the breech to load it with a .300 H&H Magnum round made specifically for his rifle. The entire royal family carried only the most expensive hunting rifles manufactured by Holland & Holland out of Britain. They were made from the finest British walnut and steel, with elaborate metal engravings decorating the stock and trigger guard.

"Do we have a direction of travel?" the king asked.

"He's been heading due south for days," DeKlerk said. "Trying to find his way home, we figure."

"Let's form up the party and begin," Leopold announced. "First, we'll have Balthazar's security people run him to ground, just like we use dogs during foxhunts. Then we'll close in and make the kill once our prey is cornered—"

Just in front of the group, the head of one of the PSD contractors suddenly snapped backward in a spray of blood.

Then they heard the gunshot.

CHAPTER

40

LOPEZ FELT THE rifle buck against his shoulder and barely heard the retort of the shot, as his mind was laser focused on the targets downrange.

He was damned tired of playing defense, of being hunted and on the run.

When he heard the approaching rotor blades, he vectored in on their sound and found the helicopter landing in a clearing not far off. Staying low and behind cover and concealment, he moved within four hundred meters of the landing zone, extended the HK 417's bipod legs, and got into the prone position.

He wasn't feeling anywhere near back to 100 percent, but the six-hour energy shot he had found in Gideon's bag certainly helped.

After riding out the recoil, Lopez let the reticle in his sniper scope return to its original position, then, by slightly twisting his torso, he aligned the cross hairs on the chest of another guy who looked like a security contractor. These men were wearing civilian clothes but had plate carriers loaded with spare magazines and AR-15 rifles held at the ready.

He didn't know who else had arrived by helicopter, but he identified the tactical team as being the biggest threat, and so he focused on them first. Lopez squeezed the trigger, and through the scope, he saw the bullet cut through the heat mirage rising off of the dry African ground before it spun around the security contractor and dropped him to the ground.

A third contractor got his rifle up and took a knee, searching for the Ranger's position. Lopez sent another shot his way. He couldn't tell where the round impacted, but the shooter suddenly keeled over onto his back. In his book, that was a clean kill.

The fourth security contractor had found cover behind a tree and was rapidly unloading in Lopez's direction, searching him out with gunfire. The suppressive fire worked, especially when the new hunters joined in, firing some kind of single-shot large-bore rifles. Elephant guns, he suspected.

Sticks and twigs from the tree above were now falling down onto him as the gunfire raked above his position and chipped away at the tree.

Lopez rolled behind the trunk of the tree with the 417 still in hand, slung it, and moved out as fast as he could in a crouch while being careful to keep the tree between himself and the clearing where the hunters were.

Gradually the shooting behind him died down, and just as fast as the attack had begun, he had withdrawn to plan his next attack.

This time, Lopez was the predator.

* * *

The twenty-something-year-old kids putted around and stared at the ground in a daze. They had each killed people before, but shooting poachers from a helicopter was one thing. Now someone had the audacity to actually shoot back at them.

It was a new and shocking development.

Astrid covered her mouth and looked away from the corpses of the security contractors, but King Leopold smiled and clapped DeKlerk on the back.

"Well done, lad, well done," he said in a jovial mood. "You found a good one."

DeKlerk looked away and back to his radio. He was going to call in Henry's PSD to back them up in the field, and he would insist that Balthazar pick up their tab. That would plus up the security team to five total, and clearly they were going to need it.

The hunt was getting dicier by the moment. What had started off seeming like a sure thing now wasn't. The Ranger had successfully turned things around and seized the initiative. DeKlerk planned to change that reversal back around once more.

CHAPTER 41

A SMALL FIRE BEGAN billowing a cloud of gray smoke as the hunting party settled in for the night.

By the time the other security team evacuated Henry's body and came back, it was nearly nightfall. They made camp, and all five contractors stood guard on the perimeter. They also put out a series of trip flares that would be impossible to detect once it got dark.

Three civilian backpacking tents had been erected, and the hunting party sat on foldable stools made for outdoorsmen. Leopold, relaxed, whittled away at what was to be a walking stick. At nearly sixty, he was a burly and generally fit fellow.

The kids still looked a little shaken up from the ambush earlier in the day, so he decided to cheer them up a bit.

"Personally, I think our family has gotten too soft," he said. "And I include myself in this, of course. Our predecessors would not have let their prey ambush them like that and then get away."

"Oh, please," Astrid chided.

"It's true," Leopold insisted before turning back to his children and son-in-law. "Did I ever tell you any of the hunting stories about grandpapa?"

They shook their heads no.

"Well then," Leopold said. "There was a time in the distant past when royal families across Europe would engage in the hunting sports, and sometimes that included the hunting of man, although it was rarer than you might think. Usually the prey was some social undesirable or pauper that everyone wanted to be rid of anyway."

He held out his handiwork in front of him for a moment, inspecting it, then continued his whittling. "The gallows or the hunt," Leopold lamented. "Your grandpapa Emmanuel came home from the war and found himself in a spot of trouble due to his close associations with prominent Germans," he continued. "He wanted to do something to bring together the Belgian elite class and reinvented this royal tradition based on stories he had in turn heard from his own grandparents. He used to host hunts with members of the Blue Salon at Château de Chimay."

"You never told us about this," said his younger son, Rudolph. The boy was on holiday from his studies at Oxford and had joined them for what had seemed would be a once-in-a-lifetime experience.

"Oh yes," the father said. "Our family has a long history with manhunts. But here is something I'm sure none of you knew," he said with a twinkle in his eye.

"Stop being coy, Papa," Josephine scolded. "Just tell us already."

"Your grandpapa also used to organize child hunts."

The entire family seemed taken aback by this new claim, causing them to sit up straight on their stools. Johann's jaw hung open, and Rudolph had a slight smirk on his face. Albert leaned forward, listening with fascination, hanging on every word.

"Your grandpapa would make a game out of it, telling the children to run and hide in the woods around the castle, and when they were discovered, he would scold them and set them loose again. When they were captured a certain number of times, they would then take out the guns. Oftentimes bows and arrows as well.

"The thing to remember is to turn the arrowheads when hunting people," he went on. "You fire the arrow so that the broadhead is horizontal to the ground; that way it can slip between a human's ribs."

Josephine listened raptly, smiling as if delighted by the tale, while the boys appeared equally enthralled.

Suddenly, gunfire ripped through the camp. Bullets snapped and popped all around the hunters as Leopold dove toward his wife and dragged her to the ground. The rest of the family hit the ground even as they heard the PSD team return fire into the wood line. DeKlerk began screaming in guttural Afrikaans.

As Leopold lay atop his wife, he turned to see Josephine lying on the ground, hugging her knees and mumbling to herself.

* * *

The low-light sniper training he had received at Fort Benning was paying off. Lopez was sure he'd tagged at least one person, probably one of the security detachment guys standing guard on the perimeter of the camp.

The dumbasses had even lit a fire, illuminating the contours of the hunters as they shuffled around the camp. After dropping the sentry he'd spied, Lopez raked the camp with the remainder of the magazine in his HK 417, making bold corrections that swept through the enemy.

Before engaging, the Ranger had spent nearly an hour on his final approach to the camp, slowly stalking forward. The camp was easy enough to identify, given the lack of noise and light discipline among this new batch of hunters. Whoever they were, they weren't used to the two-way firing range.

A trained sniper, Lopez used a technique called tree stacking. As he crept forward through the night, he made sure to keep at least one big tree trunk in front of him, between him and the camp. This offered cover if he received enemy fire but also concealed his approach. As he moved into his final firing position, he found a stack of trees to shoot between, again offering him cover. It would also make it difficult for the hunters to figure out where the gunfire was coming from due to problems in depth perception when trying to judge the shooter's position in relation to the trees he used as cover.

It hadn't taken the security team so long to figure out his general direction, though, and now he was receiving return fire. He could hear 5.56 rounds chewing into the tree trunk next to him and snapping over his head.

Ducking completely behind the tree, Lopez ejected the spent magazine in his rifle and rammed home a fresh one. His second-to-last twenty-rounder.

Keeping the tree to his back, he began to move away from the camp the same way he had approached earlier in the day. There was a temptation to assault forward, to meet the enemy eye to eye, but Lopez knew he would be throwing his life away. Not this late in the game, not when he had a chance at the prize, which was nothing less than survival.

He remembered his own initial assessment of his situation. His survival hinged on making many small but tactically sound decisions, not bold aggressive maneuvers on a force that had him outmanned and outgunned. His attack on the camp was meant to whittle down their numbers a bit and harass the survivors, depriving them of rest and forcing them to stay vigilant through the night.

More gunfire popped behind Lopez as he made his getaway deeper into the forest, but it soon faded away.

Tomorrow was another day, a day that promised combat and death.

CHAPTER 42

SPORADIC GUNFIRE PEPPERED the camp through the early-morning hours after dawn. More than once during the night, a pop flare was tripped out on the perimeter, casting long shadows through the forest.

It wasn't long after the first attack that they found one of Henry's PSD contractors face down on the perimeter with a 7.62mm hole through his sternum.

"This guy is something else," Balthazar said as the echo of the latest gunshot faded.

"Getting that long gun in his hands gave him a pinch of self-confidence," DeKlerk concluded.

The royal family was packing up camp, the now four-man PSD acting almost as porters by humping the tents and other camping gear on their backs in rucksacks. The kids looked a bit frazzled, the night of harassing gunfire having left them sleepless. King Leopold appeared in good spirits as they set out on the day's hunt.

Before they headed out, DeKlerk radioed the remaining helicopter pilot. He wouldn't let the pilot get close for fear of having another shoot-down, but he did want a bird in the sky looking for the Ranger. There was so much spoor around the perimeter of the campsite from a night of shenanigans that it was hard for even the experienced tracker to make head or tail of it.

Trails of footprints looped around on themselves, trampled over one another, and then disappeared in all directions. Acting on a hunch, DeKlerk led the hunting party south. Moving in that cardinal direction had been a constant with their prey. He understood he needed to move south to find civilization; they just had to beat him there.

The grim irony, DeKlerk noted, was that they were in such a remote part of Benin that the Ranger would have to be exceptionally fortunate to stumble across another village or a passing vehicle on a dirt road. Even if he outran the hunters, he would simply die tired due to exposure to the elements. There wasn't a town within a hundred miles.

Before midday, the hunters received word from the helicopter pilot. He had caught sight of Lopez crossing a large open field just to the southwest of their current position.

"Let's go, single file," DeKlerk ordered the hunting party.

The four PSD contractors took point, followed by DeKlerk, who was followed by the royals, with Balthazar trailing behind them. The South African intended to move them with a purpose, like a military patrol, so he put them in a line for speed of movement. He'd have them fan out as they closed in on the Ranger.

Twenty minutes later, now having picked up Lopez's spoor again, the hunters noticed that they were walking into a gulch of sorts. It was a small valley with jagged rock formations rising on either side.

"This poes is trying to lead us into a choke point," DeKlerk said as he turned to Leopold. "He wants to trap us in here for an ambush. We won't be playing that game."

"What do you suggest?"

DeKlerk craned his neck, looking at the rocks above.

"We backtrack a few hundred meters and climb up there," he said, pointing. "We should remain on the reverse slope and see if we can ambush his ambush."

Leopold smiled. He liked this idea.

It took the better part of an hour, and everyone's clothes were soaked through with sweat by the time they arrived at the top of the ridgeline. Now DeKlerk had them move into a more tactical formation. The four-man PSD formed an arrowhead shape at the head of the formation. He had the royals spread out as much as possible behind them. Balthazar looked like he was about to have a heart attack after the climb, and struggled to keep up.

The hunters crept forward now in anticipation of contact with the Ranger. The idea was that they would sneak up right behind him as he lay prone, overwatching the valley to take sniper shots at them. It was slow going when they moved with such careful deliberation, about another hour in the heat stalking through waist-high grass.

Up ahead DeKlerk spied a crevasse between two boulders facing the edge of the canyon. A perfect sniper position, from his point of view, and definitely worthy of stalking up to for closer inspection. Using hand and arm signals, he communicated his intent to Leopold and directed him to take the lead.

Nodding his head, the Belgian king moved up to the front and began stalking through the high grass toward the rock formation. With every step his heart threatened to beat out of his chest. He had been on many hunts, but never one like this.

As he stepped up to the crevasse and saw through the stalks of beige-colored grass, his Holland & Holland rifle swept across the area, searching for the Ranger.

But there was no one there, not even a depression or blade of bent grass indicating that the position had been recently occupied. Resting one hand against the rock, Leopold turned toward DeKlerk and shook his head.

He saw the South African silently mouth the word *kak*.

Ironically, standing in the location DeKlerk had identified as a superior sniper position may very well have been what saved the king's life.

Gunfire sounded from downhill, the shots coming in rapid succession. One of the PSD members collapsed to his knees and then began rolling downhill.

The bastard gave up the high ground knowing we would come, DeKlerk immediately realized. The Ranger had taken the inferior position in exchange for the element of surprise. Now he was shooting into their backs.

The other three PSD members took a knee and began laying down a base of fire while Astrid and the kids dove for cover.

"WHY IS HE SHOOTING AT US!" Josephine cried out.

The boys at least began returning fire with their H&H rifles once they had found cover behind some other boulders. Unfortunately, they had been ambushed trying to ambush an ambush and were now caught in a relatively open area.

A second PSD member pitched forward and took a long dirt nap, dead.

"This is a bloody shooting gallery," DeKlerk yelled at no one in particular. He grabbed the king of Belgium by the collar of his shirt, dragged him toward Astrid, and led the way.

"You lot, follow me. We need to clear the kill zone now!" the South African safari guide yelled.

Balthazar looked unperturbed and carefully scanned the foliage below with his sniper rifle, taking carefully aimed shots at suspected targets. Lopez was dug in like a tick, wherever he was down there.

DeKlerk got the royals in another single-file line and ran for it. The last two remaining PSD members stayed behind to lay down suppressive fire to aid their escape, while Balthazar left them behind upon seeing the others flee.

One of the PSD contractors ducked down into the high grass, changed magazines, and popped back up, sweeping from left to right with the barrel of his AR-15 while sending 5.56 rounds downhill and downrange.

Then a single shot issued from a copse of trees below, and his rifle too fell silent.

The final contractor picked up from his position and was running for it, trying to catch up with the hunting party, when a single 7.62 round plugged him just under the armpit and blasted through his rib cage and into his heart.

He was dead before he hit the ground.

CHAPTER

43

THE SECURITY CONTRACTOR stared up at the blue sky and knew that he was going to die today.

He'd been hit, tumbled forward, and rolled sideways down the hill until his body finally flopped to a stop. He was bruised, battered, shot, and bleeding out.

He heard footsteps approaching and rolled his head from side to side to see who it was. Suddenly, he was staring into intense brown eyes. They seemed to gaze right through him. Hands quickly relieved him of a fixed blade combat knife and his sidearm. His rifle and rucksack had fallen away somewhere.

The two men just looked at each other for a moment. The contractor wore MultiCam fatigues and a chest rig and looked like some kind of paramilitary guy. The man who shot him did not look too dissimilar. He too wore a fatigue jacket, boots, and a white-faced watch and cradled an HK 417 rifle in his hands.

The contractor remained silent, knowing what his fate was, but to his surprise the man spoke.

"Were you blue, green, or red?"

The contractor was taken aback by this turn of events. Those were color code names used for special operations units during the war.

"Blue," he answered. There was no reason to hold back at this point.

"Teams or SWCC?" he asked next, pronouncing the acronym *swick*.

"Teams."

"Evens or odds?"

"Evens."

"Two, four, six, eight, or ten?"

"Ten."

The man nodded.

"You were in the teams?" the contractor gasped, his breaths coming in shorter and shorter bursts.

This time the man shook his head.

"I'm with Task Force Red."

"Yeah, man. Got it. Ranger bros."

"You shouldn't be out here."

The contractor coughed up some blood. "Yeah, neither should you."

"Got that right, but it wasn't as if I was given a choice."

"Will you do something for me?"

"Probably not."

"Let me die here under the sky my own way, okay? I don't need a coup de grace. We both know this is the end of the line for me regardless."

The man appeared to consider this for a moment.

"Okay, sure."

With that, he collected up the contractor's weapons and rifled through his pockets and pouches for a few other items before he began to walk away.

"Hey," the contractor croaked.

The Ranger stopped and looked over his shoulder.

"Thank you."

The Ranger nodded.

"Before you go, there is one last thing you need to know," the contractor said, his voice getting quieter. "That weasel DeKlerk, the South African . . ."

"Yes, I know him, unfortunately."

"He's not working alone."

"What do you mean?"

"His safari has a state sponsor this time around."

"Bullshit."

"Apparently you were a real pain in the ass to them, successfully helping to target the Islamist militants that they were covertly financing as proxies in Niger. From what I overheard, you pissed off a lot of people."

The Ranger perked up at this and turned to face the ex-SEAL.

"It's the Russians. The Wagner Group."

CHAPTER 44

THE BELGIAN ROYAL family were all gasping, doubled over, clutching their knees. Johann was puking. Josephine couldn't stop shaking despite how damned hot it was.

DeKlerk had run them hard for several kilometers before he permitted them to stop on the backside of another hill he had found. Now he was yelling at them to form a security perimeter.

"Stop feeling sorry for yourselves, you lot," he scolded, the old-school paramilitary commando in him coming out.

"Give it a rest," Leopold said as he stood up tall, his chest heaving. Their shirts showed white salt stains from the amount of sweat they were all losing. "We have some time to regroup before he's able to catch up with us again."

The South African snorted before giving up on the argument and took a drink from his canteen.

Just then Balthazar came stumbling into their hasty security perimeter, finally catching up with the group.

Everyone had forgotten about him. When he arrived, he looked at the party expectantly, like he felt he deserved their attention, which never came.

"Gather around, everyone," the king commanded. "I know everyone feels just terrible right now."

"That man nearly killed us," gasped Albert, his son-in-law.

"Why was he shooting at us, Papa?" Josephine asked.

"Why, because he is the hunted, my darling little girl," Leopold answered. "The family has grown bored hunting paupers and wanted someone who was a bit of a sport."

"Those security guys," she panted. "They're dead."

"Well, yes, but we'll buy more of them."

"They were just NPCs," Balthazar said under his breath. Everyone ignored him.

"They're dead," she repeated, almost at a whisper.

"Chin up, kids, this is only a minor setback, as is to be expected on any hunt."

Balthazar dabbed his forehead with a handkerchief as his pulse returned to normal.

"We just need to get our bearings," Astrid offered.

"That's right," Leopold said. "Today is the day for our youngsters, who deserve the opportunity to attain glory in battle like the knights of old. In order to show that you are ready for leadership, you must prove so during the hunt. Show us that you are prepared to defend our race and our land."

The boys looked up at him with fury in their eyes, their bloodlust growing. They had been raised to believe that they were of "pure blood" and destined to govern the lesser, degenerate races, as their ancestors had in the Congo, Sudan, and Rwanda during the previous two centuries.

"We'll show this boy who's in charge here. These people have monkey blood in them. The blood of generations of gilded nobility runs through your veins. To rule is your destiny. Now you must reach out and take what this world owes to each of you."

"How do we kill him, Papa?" Rudolph asked.

Leopold smiled.

"We lay a trap for this tiger."

* * *

Russians.

That changed a few things.

The Wagner Group was a Russian private military company that hired all sorts of rabble, from ex-soldiers to ex-convicts to current convicts, to fight Russia's dirty wars in Syria, Ukraine, and across Africa.

Lopez had assumed that the people hunting him were sickos and freaks. Now it turned out that this was something far more serious. It was known within his circles that the Russians and Americans both sponsored proxy warfare against one another, and his chosen profession as an RRC Ranger made him an expert at it.

During the Afghanistan war, Lopez had deployed as a young infantryman before going to RRC, and from there was sent out on Omega Team deployments that fused the capabilities of the CIA and special operations into one. Those were wild days, and the Army wasn't asking any questions when the Rangers returned from running Title 50 covert operations for the CIA. They didn't know and didn't want to know.

Another mission set was the Afghanistan Reconnaissance Unit, or ARU.

RRC ran the ARU as a source network in Afghanistan using old-school tradecraft. They rarely met face-to-face with their recruited assets but outfitted them with local vehicles that were bugged with trackers and clandestine cameras, communicated via dead drops, and even sent ARU members on assassination missions, sometimes across international borders.

Lopez's primary mission in Niger had been to counter violent extremist organizations. Niger had a population that the US government considered to be vulnerable and at risk of Islamic extremism. The special operations community had been tasked with getting ahead of the problem before the place turned into another Afghanistan. It made sense. Taking Lopez and Wallaby off the chessboard stripped JSOC of their intelligence capability on the ground. No intel meant no ops, directed against Russian proxy forces or otherwise.

But what he hadn't known, and apparently neither did the Army, was that those extremists were being funded by Russia. For the Russians, it would be an opportunity to strike back against America in Africa in retaliation for their support of the Ukrainians, whom the Russians saw simply as a NATO proxy.

It was complicated and messy, and Lopez knew that while interesting, this information was of no immediate use to him. He was still fighting for his life in the African bush.

He went through the gear piled at his feet, inspecting item by item. The HK 417 was all out of ammo, and it seemed unlikely that he would find more 7.62×51 rounds in the near future, so he discarded the rifle and claimed one of the dead contractors' AR-15s instead.

After policing up as much gear from the fallen as he could, he found a place to sit and look it over for a moment. He had seen the hunting party huff it out of his kill zone as quickly as possible, and he figured they were now regrouping and coming up with a new game plan.

Lopez had a game plan of his own. Relentless pursuit. He was done playing defense.

Quickly, he sorted through the thirty-round 5.56 Magpul PMAGs for the AR. He went through and made sure that the half-empty ones were used to top off the others, discarded any empties, and jammed the full mags into a chest rig he had claimed from one of the dead contractors.

Next, he looked over the holographic reflex sight and backup iron sights on the rifle, which included a tac light with a cracked lens that still appeared functional. He also messed with the sling to make sure it fit him the way he liked.

While he worked, he gulped down bottles of water he had found on the dead men.

Unfortunately, he didn't find any night vision devices on the contractors, but he did scrounge up a few flashlights, some additional food, spare batteries, a fixed-blade knife, rain gear, and spare socks, which he was only too happy to slip onto his feet after discarding the disgusting old ones.

The spare gear went into an assault pack he had also claimed during his battlefield recovery.

He'd made short work of the paramilitary contractors, and as he shrugged into the chest rig and slung his rifle, he knew it was time to start chewing up the rest of the hunting party.

CHAPTER

45

DEKLERK WAS HELPING the royal family come up with the concept of a plan for a trap when Lopez caught up with them. Suddenly, it seemed like gunfire was coming from everywhere at once. The South African's hat was shot right off his head. One of the royals had their rifle shot out of their hands before he received a gunshot wound to his arm.

DeKlerk hit the ground and rolled behind a tree, eventually picking out from the *pop-pop-pop* on their perimeter that the gunfire was coming from their left flank. From the sound of the rifle fire, he also deduced that Lopez had ditched the semiautomatic sniper rifle for one of the contractor's AR-15s.

To their credit, both Leopold and Balthazar immediately took cover and returned fire. Balthazar worked the bolt on his .300 Win Mag sniper rifle, and the king fired .300 H&H big-game rounds downrange before popping open the breech to reload. DeKlerk realized that carrying hunting rifles against someone with a semiauto combat rifle left them outgunned. This wasn't the sporting event they had planned at all.

DeKlerk grabbed up Rudolph and Albert and got them on line with Balthazar and Leopold. Astrid, Josephine, and Johann formed a second front, and once their rifle fire joined the cacophony, DeKlerk started to maneuver the first element like an infantry unit. They were in combat now.

"Right side, bound forward ten meters!" he shouted over the gunfire.

Balthazar, Leopold, and Albert had their rifles at the ready as they bounded forward through the brush, looking for the Ranger with eager rifle muzzles.

The AR-15 fire had ceased, making DeKlerk wonder if it was finally over. Maybe one of them had smoked the Ranger.

He was about to bound Astrid's element forward when the gunfire suddenly picked up again, but from a new location.

"Cease fire!" DeKlerk screamed far too late.

* * *

Running down the hunting party had been the easy part for Lopez. They had trampled a trail like a herd of elephants. The Ranger had handrailed their spoor and moved quickly to catch up with them.

The game had changed, and his new tactical approach was relentless pursuit, never taking the pressure off the enemy.

Thinking he spotted some lateral movement through the trees, he began stepping carefully from heel to toe, moving forward as quietly as possible. Creeping forward another thirty meters, he was able to confirm movement as well as hear low voices. He could hear them clearly enough, but they were speaking a language foreign both to him and to West Africa. It sounded European, but Lopez couldn't place it.

Taking a knee next to a tree, Lopez flicked the selector switch on his AR-15 from safe to semi and looked down through his reflex sight. Seeing more movement from the hunting party to his front, Lopez opened fire.

He shot repeatedly at the target he spied through the trees, then raked gunfire back and forth across the enemy location. The return fire came faster than he had expected. Lopez flinched as a round snapped somewhere to his right-hand side.

Sticking around for a stand-up fight with the hunters was not part of the game plan, so he emptied the rest of his magazine in their direction and reloaded while peeling back into the wood line.

Running back ten meters, he hopped over a fallen tree and then ducked behind it.

To his surprise, the hunters appeared to be bounding toward him, moving forward on an assault line. DeKlerk was rallying the troops, no doubt as if they were an infantry squad.

He was about to return fire when he caught movement to his right. Through the trees he saw the redheaded woman and several others. They were bounding forward in a second element, maybe trying to flank him.

There seemed to be a relatively large separation between the two elements, making him wonder if they could effectively support one another in a firefight. Deep down, he knew these civilian hunters weren't hardened combat troops and that under stress their discipline would disintegrate.

The idea that occurred to him was a gamble, maybe reckless. Possibly suicidal.

Taking a deep breath, he gripped his rifle and bounded forward, moving diagonally to place himself between the two hunter teams. As he swept by the leading element, he pivoted and shot from the hip, spraying their line with gunfire. Then he turned and fired on the second element's position to the other side.

He wanted them to know where he was.

Then he threw himself to the ground.

Gunfire ripped through the space he had occupied just a split second ago. The sound of gunshots came from multiple directions, crisscrossing above Lopez as he high-crawled toward a tree to his front. There were shouts between the gunfire, also coming from both sides.

"Cease fire, cease fire!" he heard someone yell.

That was when Lopez popped up on a knee and returned fire, first to his left, then to his right, before pancaking himself on the ground again.

Then he listened to their discipline break down as both elements opened fire again.

He had bounded between the hunters, who had split themselves in two. Now they were firing on each other and doing his work for him. One by one, they were learning that friendly fire wasn't.

Staying low, he continued to hold his rifle in his hands while crawling forward on his knees and elbows. The gunfire went on for another half minute before petering out. Having moved another ten or fifteen meters, Lopez turned around and shot through the rest of his magazine to get them all shooting at each other again.

Of course they did, even as he could hear the South African screaming at them to stop.

Lopez smiled as he ejected the spent magazine, rammed a fresh one into the magazine well, and dropped the bolt to chamber the first round.

Staying in a crouch, he slunk off into the wood line and disappeared.

CHAPTER

46

Astrid clawed her face in anguish, digging red streaks into her flesh. Leopold grabbed her hands to try to stop her with limited success. Tears streamed down her face, but her eyes betrayed only an animalistic rage.

"What's wrong, dear?" Leopold asked, his eyes drifting in the direction that his wife had been facing.

That was when he saw a pair of booted feet nearby.

"No," he gasped.

He rushed forward and found Josephine lying in the dirt, a single shot through her chest covering her in blood the color of midnight. Her eyes were lifeless, staring into nothing.

"No! No! No!" he heard a disembodied voice screaming, not realizing it was his own.

Leopold held his daughter in his arms and slapped her face, trying to get her to wake up. Astrid's screeching carried through the forest.

"You can't die," the king said. "I won't allow it. This cannot happen."

Just then Albert came crashing through the brush.

"Did any of you see which direction he went—"

His words ground to a halt as he saw his father-in-law cradling the body of his wife. He rushed to her side and cupped her face, smearing blood across her skin.

"She's . . . she's . . ." the king said, his voice broken and uneven. "She's gone."

The prince of Liechtenstein released his hold on his late wife, backing away from her, his eyes as wide as saucers. Then he looked down at his hands and saw them wet with Josephine's blood.

Suddenly, his eyes darted in the direction the Ranger had gone. Grabbing his rifle in hand, the prince ran at a dead sprint into the forest before anyone could stop him.

DeKlerk stood behind the king. He had watched the entire scene in silence. He flinched upon hearing a voice behind him.

"Well, that didn't go well."

DeKlerk turned and eyeballed Balthazar.

"No shit."

"Well, if they didn't like that, they're going to hate what comes next."

"What's that?"

Balthazar cleared his throat.

"This way," he said, motioning with his chin.

Balthazar led him through the area where the firefight had occurred, where Lopez had escaped and evaded, until they walked right up onto another body.

It was one of the sons, Rudolph. His brother, Johann, was trying to plug the holes in him with bandages, but it was already too late. He was dead.

"They bloody shot each other," DeKlerk hissed.

"Appears so," Balthazar said. "What a shame."

* * *

Lopez jogged through the African bush country at a steady pace, crossing over a red clay dirt road. He hoped that meant he was getting closer to civilization, although he had jettisoned his escape plan in exchange for his attack plan.

He canted his head once he was on the other side of the road, thinking he heard something unusual before continuing on. He had already moved about a kilometer from the hunters and was starting to think about looping back around on their position to continue his harassment campaign when he heard a branch snap behind him.

Turning around, he saw one of the hunters barreling down on him. He fired his rifle at Lopez, but his shot was hopelessly inaccurate. He kept charging forward, now gripping the rifle barrel like a club. His guttural scream carried through the forest.

With the hunter no more than fifteen meters from him, Lopez brought his rifle to the high ready position and fired a single shot before the AR-15 malfunctioned. The hunter flinched but kept coming.

Acting from the muscle memory created by untold hours of training on Farnsworth Range at Fort Benning, Lopez immediately indexed the Glock 19 holstered on his hip and drew it in one clean, smooth movement.

He fired once, then twice from the hip as he brought the weapon up in front of him in a modified weaver stance while the rifle hung across his chest on its sling, his eye catching the front site post and aligning it with the rear site. He squeezed the trigger and the pistol barked, once, twice, three times, then more.

He fired the first shot center mass, then walked his shots up toward the head.

Then the hunter collided with him, and they both spilled to the forest floor. Lopez went into a roll and ended up on his side with the Glock held in front of him, prepared to shoot from a prone position.

But the hunter was lying face-first in the dirt without moving.

Standing back up, the Ranger kept his pistol trained on the assailant before rolling him over with a booted foot. Eyes stared up at him, empty and vacant. Dead.

He quickly holstered his pistol and cleared the malfunction in his rifle, a double feed that was easily corrected.

Lopez knelt to take a closer look at the body. He wore expensive outdoors clothing. He had good nails, pearly white teeth, what looked like an expensive stylish haircut. On his wrist was a Rolex watch.

Who the fuck is this guy? Lopez wondered.

Walking over to where he'd dropped his rifle, Lopez picked it up and examined it. It was clearly a high-end custom-built hunting rifle, but beyond that he was unable to identify it. He dealt with military weapons, not some shit you'd expect to find British pheasant hunters shooting. The inlaid detail work on the steel plating was impressive, he had to admit. The wooden stock appeared to be made of walnut.

This was clearly a different crew than the first one he had gone up against, who reeked of Silicon Valley and hedge fund scumbags, the type of people who foreclosed on old ladies' houses and threw them out on the street. This guy was different, like some kind of blue blood. Now he wondered what language it was that he had heard them speaking earlier.

Lopez went back to the corpse and made a closer search of the body, finding a wallet in the back pocket. He also found a pendant, worn around the neck on a golden chain. He didn't recognize the symbols on it.

It looked like some weird occult shit to him. The pendant appeared to be made of some weird metal in the shape of a triangle. In the center of it, what looked like a human eye had been etched into it.

In the wallet were a bunch of European credit cards, a Swiss bank card, some other pocket litter, and finally an actual ID card in the wallet.

The name on the ID was Albert Maximillian Josef Von Mises.

It was issued by the Principality of Liechtenstein.

"What the fuck is Liechtenstein?" Lopez asked aloud.

CHAPTER

47

LEOPOLD HELD HIS wife's head into his shoulder as she cried. The bodies of two of their children lay at their feet, covered with rain ponchos.

"This can't be real," she said softly between her tears.

"Hush now, my dear, we'll get them home now."

She put both hands on his chest and pushed him away. Her face was red with sadness and rage.

"No you will not," she said.

"Will not what?"

"We are not going home. You will kill him, you will kill the American. You have to do this now. This isn't one of your sports or games; this is your duty to this family."

"Our children died gloriously in battle," the king countered. "It was perhaps their destiny."

Walking up to her husband, she grabbed him by the collar of his shirt.

"You kill him or put that barrel of your rifle in your mouth and pull the trigger," she hissed.

Leopold's eyebrows went up. He had never heard Astrid speak like this before.

"As you wish, my dear."

Leopold opened the breech on his rifle and reloaded.

"That Ranger can't have gotten far."

Just then a torrent of gunfire opened up nearby, sending Leopold and his wife back to hug the forest floor once again. Balthazar and DeKlerk stepped right over them as they moved to face the threat. The Ranger hadn't wasted any time circling back around on them.

Leopold gritted his teeth, angry at being upstaged by the South Africans. Grabbing his rifle, he chased after them. Just moments after Leopold left the clearing, his remaining son, Johann, came running by to join the other hunters.

"No, wait!" Astrid cried out. She couldn't lose another of her boys, the last to carry on the family's ancient bloodline.

But it was too late, as Johann disappeared into the foliage amid another round of gunfire.

* * *

Time to even the odds.

He knew he wouldn't be able to creep right up on their position with the entire hunting party certainly alerted to his presence from his previous attack just minutes ago, but it was still an opportunity to hit them again and keep them off-balance.

The first human form he saw through the wood line was maybe twenty-five meters to his front. He aimed and squeezed off a half dozen rounds, but the tree limbs and brush probably deflected or fragmented his rounds.

Two hunters responded almost immediately, returning fire on his position, muzzle flashes announcing their reaction from close range.

Lopez broke contact, heading back to his six o'clock position, ducking and weaving between the trees for a hundred meters and then abruptly changing direction and moving back toward the hunters again.

He ran up on their position again just moments later. The Ranger felt a surge of energy course through his veins. It felt good to be the hunter again. As he got closer, he slowed his breathing and began creeping forward more deliberately, willing himself not to rush into the situation.

Slowly, he worked his way forward. Up ahead he could hear shouts and even the occasional gunshot as the hunters sought him out. Maybe DeKlerk was doing some recon by fire to try to bait him out; that or the hunters were broken and panic-shooting in any direction.

Then, through the waist-high brush, he saw one of the hunters walking straight toward him, his eyes alert and scanning the wood line. Lopez brought the AR-15 stock into the pocket of his shoulder and looked down his EOTech holographic reflex sight. The red reticle came to a rest on the hunter's chest.

Thumbing off the safety, he gently squeezed the trigger twice in rapid succession. The hunter was thrown backward, mostly due to a parasympathetic reaction to the shock of being shot. His arms went into the air as he dropped his rifle and collapsed backward.

Lopez was panning the barrel of his rifle from left to right and back again, scanning for more targets, when a tree just a few inches in front of him seemed to explode. White bark went flying in all directions.

Instinctually, Lopez pivoted off his left foot and executed an abrupt right turn that moved his body ninety degrees to his side.

A red-haired woman stood mere meters from him, struggling with the breech of her rifle as she attempted to reload.

Lopez shot her in the face with a controlled pair of 5.56 rounds and moved on before her body had even come to a complete rest on the forest floor.

Two down.

Lopez was about to break contact again and pull a fade when he saw something near the dead woman. There were two more bodies, which had been covered in rain ponchos. Some quick battlefield math led the Ranger to conclude that there could only be two or three hunters left.

Hearing approaching footsteps crashing through the brush, Lopez froze and waited. In seconds an older figure appeared, holding a rifle in his hands. His face looked ghastly white as he saw the three bodies.

Then he saw Lopez emerging from the forest like a jungle cat, a panther about to strike.

The older man threw down his rifle and put his hands in the air.

"I surrender," he said. "I am unarmed; you cannot kill me. The laws of chivalry prevent it."

Lopez looked at what had to be a wealthy big-game hunter, one who had taken what appeared to be his family on a hunting trip—a trip to hunt him specifically.

As a member of the Ranger Regiment, Lopez was bound by American military law and the Geneva Conventions. Discipline in combat was paramount. But this wasn't war and the hunter was not a uniformed enemy soldier surrendering on the battlefield. He wasn't even a terrorist who, while misguided, ostensibly fought for a cause.

No, the old man was nothing more than a murderer who hunted human beings purely to satisfy his own vanity. He was an evil that had to be confronted.

Lopez brought his rifle into play.

"The only law out here is jungle law," Lopez said.

The hunter put his hands up in front of him as if they would stop bullets and began to shout something, but it was already too late.

Lopez shot him twice in the chest. He staggered backward, clutching his chest, as blood ran between his fingers. The Ranger shot him again, this time right on the bridge of his nose, dropping the hunter to the ground dead.

Only the fittest shall survive.

It had been a rout. His tactics had worked. Nickel-and-diming the hunters had given him small victories that appeared to be leading to a big win.

A gunshot cracked and nearly tore the rifle out of Lopez's hands. He moved to return fire from the direction he thought the shot had come from. The AR-15 chirped once and then locked back on an empty chamber, which didn't make sense, because he'd had a full magazine going in.

Ducking behind a tree, he ejected the magazine from his rifle and saw what the problem was. The hunter's shot had actually sheared through his plastic PMAG, taking with it the internal spring mechanism that fed the rounds into the gun.

Gunfire raked his position, shot after shot from a high-caliber rifle, while he quickly reloaded the rifle. Popping back up on a knee, Lopez returned fire at the enemy points of origin with his rifle as he swept fire through the forest to his front.

The large-bore rifle replied, the bullet zipping so close to his right-hand side that Lopez felt his shirtsleeve move as it passed by. Then a second rifle entered the chorus of gunfire, and the Ranger knew it was time to cut bait and make a run for it.

Leaning from behind the tree, he fired off another fusillade of gunshots to cover his withdrawal, then ran back into the forest as fast as his feet could carry him.

CHAPTER

48

IT WAS NEARING dusk when Lopez picked up the trail.

He had repeated the same maneuver he already had several times that day, retreating to a covered and concealed position and then doubling back and finding a new route to the contact location. The sun was hanging low in the sky when he walked back up on the five bodies from earlier.

For a moment he looked into their faces. He knew he probably shouldn't. People saw all kinds of things in the dead, things that weren't there. What Lopez saw was a cadaver, something that was no longer human. As ants crawled across the eyes of the dead, the only message communicated was the finality of death. He turned away and continued his search.

Moving away from the bodies, he searched for the final two guns that had fired on him. Bending a tree branch out of his way, what Lopez found instead was a blood trail. He had tagged at least one of them.

The earth in that area was disturbed, as if someone had rolled around on the leaves and dirt; then there was a very clear trail of blood heading off in a northerly direction. By his count the only two left were Balthazar and DeKlerk. Which one was it?

Lopez followed the blood trail through the brush, searching for his target.

* * *

What the Ranger didn't know was that he had accurately swept his rifle fire through the foliage and right across the position where DeKlerk and Balthazar were standing.

DeKlerk had been shot and ran off into the wood line, clutching his arm with his rifle slung over his shoulder. Balthazar felt one of his legs being swept out from under him and fell sideways, landing hard on the ground and losing control of his .300 Win Mag, rifle which fell from his hands.

The South African reached for his rifle and rolled onto his back, sure that the Ranger was about to come charging through the forest like an angry water buffalo to finish him off.

But that moment never came.

The shooting had stopped.

Balthazar lay there covered in sweat and blood.

"That can't be real," he said, looking down at his leg. His pant leg was soaked through with blood. And yet his hand came away with the viscous red liquid on it after he touched his pants.

With a groan, he used the rifle as a cane. Pressing the buttstock into the dirt, he gripped the barrel and used it to push himself back up on his feet. When he put pressure on his leg, it burned, but it did hold his weight, even if he felt weak and unsteady. The bullet hadn't gone through the bone or probably any major artery, or he would have been dead already.

He continued to use the rifle as a cane as he hobbled forward, going somewhere, anywhere to get away from the Ranger. Balthazar moved as quickly as possible, which wasn't quick at all. He was losing stamina fast.

Breaking brush, he knew he was loud as he smashed through the foliage, and was somewhat relieved to emerge out into the open savanna. An orange sun was slowly descending beneath the tree line on the horizon.

Balthazar squinted against the sun, looking around to see if he could spot DeKlerk. His fellow South African was his ticket out of this hellhole. Like it or not, he needed medical attention.

Glancing over his shoulder once, he began limping out into the savanna. He knew he had to keep moving. He gritted his teeth and focused on putting one foot in front of the other.

For a moment he thought he heard some animals moving among the underbrush, but he ignored them and kept moving, using the rifle to help him limp along. The final sliver of sun was disappearing, and he knew it would soon be dark.

"Balthazar!"

He turned at the sound of his name.

"DeKlerk? Where the fuck have you been?" he shouted back.

Suddenly, his leg shot out from under him for a second time and he collapsed to the ground.

He winced against the burning pain in his leg. He looked down to see a second splotch of blood growing on his pant leg. Hearing movement in the bushes, he reached for his rifle.

He got his hand on it just as Lopez came stalking through the tall grass. Lopez kicked the rifle out of Balthazar's reach.

"You . . . you shot me!" Balthazar exclaimed, as if shocked by this development.

"Twice," the Ranger said. He stood in front of Balthazar, the barrel of his rifle pointed downward toward his face.

"This isn't real. You don't exist. You're just an NPC."

"Nonplayer character? Like in a video game?"

"In this video game, in this simulation."

Some movement in the bushes somewhere out beyond Balthazar caught the Ranger's attention for a moment, his eyes darting into the savanna before coming back to him.

"Whatever you say, pal. This is the ultimate PvP server, I guess."

"No, no, no. You cannot do this. It's not in your programming. You're not high status; you're not even a real person. You don't exist," Balthazar repeated, almost trying to will a new reality into being.

"I do exist, Balthazar," the Ranger said. "I realize you don't know anything about me, but I exist because war exists. Nothing is real if war isn't. The scale, the tragedy, fighting and dying alongside other young men. It is all horrifyingly real, but you wouldn't understand that. Combat proves that I exist."

Balthazar's lips curled into a snarl.

"I call upon Mommojol! I call on you, Tutagool! I call out to you, Katak the Desolator!"

"The fuck you talking about?"

"The lemurs. The time demons," Balthazar said, looking about for their presence but finding that the artificial intelligences from a temporal future that hadn't happened yet were not coming to his rescue.

"Oh, so that stuff Gold was babbling about before I killed him."

"This is not real," Balthazar said, suddenly breaking into a bout of laughter.

Lopez saw mania in his eyes. This was a person who wasn't living on the same planet he was. He had fish eyes. Something was missing from them.

"There is one way to prove that this is real and not a simulation," Lopez posited.

"What could you possibly have up your sleeve that you think you can escape the annihilation of time?"

"If you, the player character in this simulation of yours, was to die, like really die, that would demonstrate that you're actually in base reality."

"As if you're the first person to think of this. Likely your coding prevents you from actually killing me."

"Not my coding," Lopez said as he fired two shots into Balthazar's good leg.

The South African tech mogul cried out in a fresh wave of pain and terror.

"That must feel pretty real, huh?"

"Fuck you!"

Lopez squatted down next to Balthazar.

"I think I'm going to follow my coding after all."

"What does that mean?" Balthazar asked through gritted teeth.

"I'm not going to kill you."

"I told you, you can't. Your programing directives won't let you. I've summoned the lemurs."

"I've got something better for you," Lopez said, standing up and grabbing Balthazar by the collar. Lopez walked, dragging him behind and changing his direction 180 degrees so he faced out into the savanna.

"I'm going to show you a reality you won't be able to deny," the Ranger said as he clasped the South African's shoulder.

"What does that even mean?" Balthazar sneered.

Lopez pointed into the tall grass.

"Look there," he said. "It's all real. All of it."

Balthazar looked over at him, but the Ranger was already walking away, taking his sniper rifle with him.

"What the fuck," he said, grasping at his legs. They burned and bled, but the pain wasn't excruciating, not yet.

Then he heard something in the grass. He looked up and squinted in the failing light, as the sun had dipped just beneath the horizon. He was about to forget about the noise until he heard it again. Then he saw the grass sway.

Something was in the grass, and it was getting closer.

Then he saw a feline face emerge. Large glass eyes leered at him, framed by pointed ears and whiskers. Another female lion appeared beside it, her face also seeming to materialize from the shadows.

Balthazar began scooting backward, leaving a trail of blood behind him. The lions crept out from the grass, and he could see how massive each of their paws was.

"Fuck. Get the fuck away!"

Beside the two females, two juvenile lions trotted out of the grass behind them. Balthazar reached for a rock and threw it in the direction of the pride of lions. One of them ducked her head and avoided the rock, which fell harmlessly into the grass.

The eyes of two hunters and two students eager to learn gazed at him as they closed in.

When he felt the lion's jaws clench around his skull, Balthazar's screams lit up the night.

CHAPTER

49

THE FARTHER SOUTH they traveled, the greener and lusher the environment had become as the savannah slowly transitioned from the Sahel in the north to the jungles in the south. DeKlerk handrailed a stream, sometimes jumping right into the water itself, in order to move quickly away from the site of the massacre.

The sound of Balthazar's screams off in the distance haunted him, and propelled him forward.

The South African ran into the night, following the stream up into a rocky draw that turned into a valley. He had to get away from the Ranger before he could call in the helicopter and get the hell out of this cursed bush country.

A full moon cast eerie shadows among the trees until they thinned out as he headed uphill and the stream flowed quickly downhill and turned into a tumbling waterfall somewhere up ahead. It was dangerous to move at night, even with night vision equipment, which he did not have, but there was no way he could stop and rest, not with Lopez somewhere out there hunting for him.

DeKlerk's legs strained as he trod uphill, stumbling several times on the rocks.

The South African did not process emotions particularly well. Having been raised within a strict Protestant patriarchal hierarchy was one reason. Years of combat and posttraumatic stress were another. He often didn't know what he was feeling, or why he was feeling it, outside of the exhilaration of combat. Until now, anyway.

Through his own fear and exhaustion, he had to admit to himself that he felt some level of admiration for the young Ranger. He had cut through both hunting parties despite being outmanned and outgunned. DeKlerk's mentoring and advice to the hunters seemed to have helped them very little. It was no great loss, of course; both groups of hunters were dandies ill-suited to the harsh reality of the bush.

They had been clients, not friends, after all.

The Ranger had shown his grit, demonstrated some level of leadership ability by inspiring the villagers to fight back against militants, and used effective fieldcraft to elude the hunters before eventually turning the tables on them. So yes, there was admiration for him. Also respect.

He'd still kill the Ranger without a second thought, but at the moment he felt like a victim of his own creation.

The approach grew steeper, forcing DeKlerk to slow his pace and move carefully, often hand over hand, as he found purchase on the rocks. Up above, he could hear the waterfall, and it looked as though the draw broke off into a small valley system beyond, likely flooded with more pools of water fed by the waterfalls.

He never saw the impact of the shot, but he heard the snap followed by the retort of a muzzle blast a second later. Flattening himself behind one of the rocks, he estimated with some very rough math, based on the time between the snap and the sound of the rifle in the distance, that the Ranger was still a ways off, maybe a thousand meters down at the bottom of the approach. DeKlerk had likely skylined himself numerous times and given away his position on a nearly full-illum night.

The second thing he surmised was that Lopez was shooting Balthazar's .300 Win Mag rifle.

Glancing from behind the rock, he scanned below and saw nothing but darkness. Using the scope on his own rifle, he probed into the night, still not finding anything, and knew he never would unless he caught sight of a muzzle flash. The Ranger was well concealed in the forest below.

Staying low to avoid silhouetting himself against the night sky, DeKlerk continued to tread uphill across rocks made slippery with water from the stream that gurgled downhill. It wasn't like he had any other option available. As he was reaching the first waterfall, another shot sounded behind his back, the round appearing to strike a rock in front of him.

Lopez kept missing, DeKlerk assumed, because he was making a difficult uphill shot at night with a rifle that had been zeroed by someone else, and he didn't have any data on the gun to help him adjust for windage and elevation and make corrections.

DeKlerk also knew his luck wasn't going to hold out forever.

One more shot went over his head as he crested the hilltop and emerged near a ten-foot waterfall that plummeted down into a small pool of water that fed the stream. Now that he had a chance of finding some good cover and had an elevated position, he paused to try to get a bead on the Ranger.

Using one of the large rock formations at the opening that led into the waterfall, he extended the bipod legs on his rifle and got down behind the scope. He had only one route to utilize as he moved uphill, and so would Lopez.

He lay in wait. Clouds drifted in front of the moon, and a light rain began to fall.

When a sniper is on glass for a long period of time, his eyes start to burn out. DeKlerk was just beginning to feel that strain in the muscles around his eyes when he spotted movement below. He scanned with the 10x scope and saw it again. Five hundred meters or so downhill. Definitely human, walking upright.

But Lopez had been making difficult shots at night, and now so was DeKlerk. It was harder to see as the moon became overcast. The South African dialed in his elevation on the scope and estimated a wind hold.

The next time he saw a flash of lateral movement below, he cranked off a shot. The round barreled downhill and disappeared. It was impossible for him to determine if he had scored a kill or not. At least it was until he saw more movement a few minutes later. The Ranger was slowly picking his way uphill toward him.

DeKlerk waited to catch movement in his scope again and squeezed off another shot. This time, a reply came right away. A bullet zinged off the rock he was taking cover behind, the muzzle flash giving away the Ranger's position in the rocks below.

DeKlerk gritted his teeth, put the reticle of his scope right over where he had seen the muzzle flash, and pulled the trigger. The Ranger answered again, this time his shooting becoming more precise as he homed in on the South African's position. The American's rifle shot kicked up dust and dirt into his face as it ricocheted off a rock just in front of him.

"*Kak*," DeKlerk muttered as he crawled backward with his rifle back behind the rock formation. He had survived enough dirty little bush wars to know when to break contact. They were trading fire, going shot for shot, until someone scored. It seemed like Lopez's fire was becoming more accurate, but it wasn't so clear if his was.

Folding the bipod legs, he slung the rifle and looked at the waterfall in front of him, trying to figure out how to scale up one of its rocky sides.

CHAPTER

50

THE CAT-AND-MOUSE GAMES carried on into the mountains and through the night.

The canyon seemed to spiderweb outward in an array of draws and passages once DeKlerk scaled the cliffs and moved deeper into the mountain. Water seeped down over the rocks from the streams above, making them slick to the touch.

DeKlerk edged along a rocky outcropping that created a small ledge that wrapped around one of the giant boulders. Glancing down, he could see the tops of trees about twenty feet below. Who knew how much farther down the gorge went after that.

Gripping the stone behind him, he shuffled around the edge and arrived on the other side. He had been keeping an eye out for a choke point that Lopez would be forced to traverse through. All DeKlerk would have to do was set up somewhere nearby with his rifle and shoot once the Ranger came scooting around the bend on the ledge.

The sun was starting to come up, and the South African was beginning to feel the effects of sleep deprivation, including some of the brain fog that came with it. It had been a long night climbing up the side of one ravine and then another. He also knew he was getting dehydrated because of the cramps he was feeling in his legs.

Following a winding lane that could scarcely be described as a footpath, maybe a goat path, DeKlerk continued along the edge of the ravine while slowly ascending once more. Up ahead he could see the waterfall that dropped down out of the cliffs, passed his elevation, and descended into the gorge.

As the goat path dissolved into the rugged rocky side of the ravine, he began to climb again, launching himself from one boulder to the next. As he leapt onto a flat piece of rock the size of a manhole cover, the ground beneath it suddenly gave way. He reached out to grab on to the rocky ledge to avoid falling, and it was only decades of combat experience that allowed him to instinctively grapple to keep his rifle, preventing it from tumbling away.

His rifle was his lifeline in this most dangerous game.

Catching his breath, the South African continued upward. The sun wasn't even fully up yet, and he was already sweating through his shirt. Minutes later, he arrived at the waterfall and took refuge within the green vegetation surrounding it. He moved as deep as he could into the foliage, utilizing it for concealment while he went prone with his rifle and sighted on the narrow cliff ledge he had previously identified. He was also practicing warfare 101 by keeping the rising sun to his back.

The Ranger wasn't that far behind him, maybe only half an hour or so away in this difficult terrain. DeKlerk readjusted his wide-brimmed hat on his head as he gazed through his rifle scope, watching for movement. He must have been on glass for about twenty minutes when he came off for a moment to rub his eyes.

As he opened his eyes and put his cheek back on the buttstock, he saw it.

A glint off something, a reflection of sunlight on the ridge across from him as the sunlight rose behind him and cast itself on the rocks. Then the first round screamed in and took a piece of meat out of his shoulder, blasting open his shirt in the process.

The South African didn't feel it yet. He shifted his position, aiming at the ridge where he'd seen the glint of the morning sun reflecting off something, and squeezed the trigger. He didn't feel any pain but knew it would come. Now he was focused, working the bolt again and again as he squeezed off rounds, aiming for the sniper on the opposite ridge.

Fucking Lopez had found an alternate route following a parallel track rather than trailing directly behind him like he had earlier during the night.

A second .300 Win Mag round smashed into a small sapling next to DeKlerk, completely severing it and sending it toppling on top of him. DeKlerk had seen a muzzle flash this time, maybe four hundred meters away, and returned fire.

A third round impacted just in front of him, spraying his face with dirt.

They were trading fire again, both from dug-in positions, but Lopez had an elevation advantage, although he was staring into the rising sun. Still, it was only a matter of time before the next round came, probably the final one that would end his life.

Retreating backward was impossible; he'd be killed while trying to climb the ridge. The only escape was forward. DeKlerk sprang to his feet, rolling the sapling off his back and charging forward. His heart threatened to beat right out of his chest as he dashed forward toward the waterfall, coming up over the rocks, expecting the shot that would kill him at any moment.

His feet left the rocks as he flung himself forward and he was airborne, holding his rifle out in front of him. The sides of the ravine screamed passed him, and what looked like little trees below suddenly rose up to meet him as they grew in size.

Then all he could see was muddy brown water taking up the full horizon of his vision.

* * *

Forty minutes later, Lopez stood at the head of the waterfall where he had watched DeKlerk jump. Looking down, he saw that the drop was about fifty feet. He thought he made out footprints on the muddy banks of the water pool below and confirmed them by looking through the scope on the .300 Win Mag.

Fucking unbelievable. Lopez had only two five-round magazines for the .300 Win Mag and had expended both. Just as he was transitioning back to his AR-15 rifle, DeKlerk had decided to YOLO right off the side of the cliff. It was a ballsy move, no doubt about it, and one that seemed to have paid off for him, since Lopez had had him trapped like a rat.

He set the sniper rifle down. Without any ammunition for it, the weapon was of little use to him. The AR-15 would have to do, along with the two thirty-round magazines he had left for it. Unslinging the rifle, he held it in front of him.

The Ranger didn't look down. Ironically, the paratrooper had a problem with heights.

He took a deep breath. Then he stepped off and fell.

CHAPTER

51

DEKLERK HAD HIT the water hard, then sank down to the bottom of the muddy pool before he was able to kick his way to the surface. His gamble had paid off. The Ranger was somewhere on the ridge far above him, unable to find him among the trees and vegetation separating them. At the bottom of the ravine, it was almost thick enough to be a jungle.

He swam to the muddy banks and lifted himself out of the water. His small assault pack and other gear were now waterlogged, as was his rifle, his lifeline, which he had never let slip from his grasp for even an instant. Thankfully, the electronics in his bag, such as the satellite phone and radio he would need to call for the helicopter, were in a waterproof bag.

For a moment he considered lying up in another ambush position, but discounted it. Lopez always had the chance of potentially sussing out his position again, and again firing upon him from with the high-ground advantage. No, better to evade and find a better location.

Trudging through the mud, he quickly disappeared into the forest and pushed himself hard, running to put as much space between himself and the Ranger as possible. He only made a brief tactical pause, just long enough to put a field bandage on his bloody shoulder wound. It was bleeding profusely and was beginning to hurt like hell, especially as the shoulder strap on his pack put pressure on it.

It was slowing him down. His feet were dragging as he came out into the mouth of the ravine and the ground began sloping back downhill. He staggered back into the savannah, surrounded within a cathedral of tree trunks that spiraled up into the African sky.

The exit from the ravine was another natural choke point, one he would be able to take advantage of. The South African didn't have much gas left in the tank, and he knew it. This was going to be his last opportunity to finish off the American.

Wincing against the pain, he began his movement, leaving a clear trail of spoor in his wake.

* * *

Lopez surfaced in what felt like an explosion of energy as he kicked upward and gasped for air.

He swam for the shore, coming to the same point where DeKlerk had surfaced mere minutes ago. His boot prints and even a few handprints were perfectly visible in the mud where he had clambered out of the water and into the woods.

Swimming to where he could stand, Lopez scanned the wood line with his AR-15 rifle, wary of another ambush. The AR could survive a dunk in the water and should still fire, but it would still require some cleaning. Right now he knew he had to clear out of the water.

He ran right over DeKlerk's tracks and up into the woods. Once within the cover and concealment provided by the dense vegetation at the bottom of the ravine, he made a quick security halt to look, listen, and smell for signs of the enemy. Beyond a clear spoor trail left behind by the South African, he observed nothing out of place.

He knew the AR-15 would need to be fieldstripped and cleaned, but he dared not do so when he could be actively engaged in combat at any moment.

Picking up DeKlerk's trail was easy. He was dragging his feet, and then not far along Lopez detected a beaten-down area where he had sat down. Judging by some of the blood on the surrounding leaves, he had clearly been injured. Lopez might have tagged him after all, but it remained to be seen how serious the injury was.

DeKlerk was hurt but not out of the game. In some ways, it could make the South African more dangerous, as he was now a cornered, wounded animal. Desperation could set in and cause a person to make brash decisions they wouldn't normally make. It was an inclination Lopez had battled himself throughout the entire ordeal.

Lopez slowed his pace and moved cautiously, quietly, pushing his senses out into the forest, searching for signs of life. This was the end game, he knew. DeKlerk, of course, would have made the same inference by now.

Minutes later, he emerged out of the ravine and into the forest once more. The sun was rising in the clear blue sky. Lopez knew that if nothing else, he would be somewhere beautiful when he died. Maybe that was the best a soldier could hope for.

The ground here was soft and spongy, either from spring water or recent rainfall, and left a clear trail of footprints for Lopez to follow. The South African was now like a freight train moving through the jungle, dragging his feet and stumbling around. He was either severely injured or trying to lull Lopez into a trap by using deception.

Massive trees created a sprawling canopy above, casting cool shadows below as the terrain opened up some and allowed faster travel. Lopez continued to move forward cautiously for several kilometers until he noticed that the footprints were slowly altering course, moving in a large half-moon.

Was DeKlerk doglegging back on his trail for an ambush? No, it wouldn't make sense. If so, DeKlerk would have ambushed him before he actually reached the change in direction of travel so as to maintain the element of surprise.

Over the course of an hour, the Ranger followed the path as it looped back around the way they had both come, but there was still no sign of DeKlerk's presence aside from his recent passage. Eventually, the half-moon was complete and Lopez arrived at their original spoor near the exit of the ravine.

He continued stalking forward. trying to find DeKlerk's direction of travel after he crossed over both of their original spoor trails. That was when he saw it.

First, there were DeKlerk's footprints as they moved from the ravine into the forest, which he had followed. Then there were Lopez's footprints as he had tracked DeKlerk from the mouth of the ravine into the forest. But to his shock and surprise, Lopez now saw a third set of footprints to his front paralleling the first two, tracking them.

Lopez spun on the ball of his foot to conduct an about-face and dropped down to a knee as his rifle automatically snapped up and into action. DeKlerk fired first, his gunshot streaking passed Lopez's face even as he was already returning fire.

With his reticle lined up on the South African's chest, Lopez stroked the trigger twice and watched him stagger and fall backward.

"Motherfucker," Lopez said under his breath, surprised to be alive.

The South African had been the one tracking him all along. From the time he had exited the ravine, he'd lain in wait, then stalked and hunted him like a tiger. Lopez had only pieced it together at literally the last second.

Now blood was running down his face, and he knew that he had been hit. Not bad enough to kill him, not yet.

Lopez charged forward, his rifle leading the way as he came up on DeKlerk's prostrate form.

"I can't believe you fucking ducked my shot, Yank," the South African cursed.

Lopez kept the muzzle of his rifle pointed at his chest. DeKlerk's hunting rifle lay at his feet, having fallen from his grasp. His lifeline was drawing to a rapid close. Lopez's two shots had created a blossom of crimson that was slowly spreading across DeKlerk's field shirt.

"I see it now," the South African said as he let his head rest on the ground, on a natural cushion of green moss.

"See what?" Lopez asked.

"You're the tiger that hunts tigers."

A wheeze escaped the South African's lips, and his chest stopped heaving. Lopez stepped forward and saw his lifeless eyes staring up at the forest canopy.

End game.

CHAPTER

52

Nick le Hanie cranked the engine on his Sikorsky helicopter as quickly as possible. The moment the call had come in, the camp had exploded in a flurry of activity. They hadn't heard from the hunting party in days.

Then the Iridium phone went off and Balthazar Botha was on the line panicking and saying that DeKlerk was seriously injured but alive. The American was finally dead. They needed to bring the body in to get paid the bounty on him, and De Klerk needed medical attention.

As the shaft on the helicopter's engine began spinning the rotor blades, one of the remaining PSD contractors in the camp jumped on board to assist with the evac. He was a medic and carried an aid bag slung over one shoulder.

With the contractor giving him a thumbs-up, Nick took off and nosed them toward the reported location of the hunting party. They had a series of predesignated landing zones in what DeKlerk had termed the "contact area," which were marked on their maps. He was now flying out to LZ 3A for the pickup. It was only a twenty-five-minute flight from the camp to the LZ as Nick gunned it all the way there at max speed, not even bothering to do a flyby to inspect the LZ before coming in for a landing.

A few hundred meters away, he was surprised to see DeKlerk waving to them. If he was injured, he was at least up on his feet. It was clearly him in his wide-brimmed hat. As the helicopter landed and DeKlerk came trotting up to the bird, Nick could see blotches of red blood on his clothes.

The contractor hopped out of the cab of the helicopter and jogged toward DeKlerk. Then Nick saw the medic go down on his knees and collapse. DeKlerk covered the remaining twenty meters, flung open the passenger door on the helicopter, and climbed in while the pilot was too stunned to react.

DeKlerk had a Glock in his hand pointed directly at the pilot. It wasn't until he was able to pry his attention away from the muzzle of the pistol that Nick realized that in fact it was not his old South African war buddy Koos DeKlerk. It was the American, his eyes wild and crazy, staring straight through him.

"You're the pilot," the American screamed over the sound of the rotor wash. "So fly this fucking thing."

He didn't have to be told twice. He pulled up on the collective and the helicopter rose, allowing a clear view of the PSD medic lying face-first in the grass. Now it was clear that he had been shot dead. The American took off

DeKlerk's hat and rested it on his knee before pulling the headset hanging behind his head over his ears. The Glock never wavered away from the pilot.

Glancing over, Nick saw that the American had indeed been injured. A slick of slowly congealing blood ran down the side of his face and onto his neck.

After realizing that he had been flying in a random direction for a few minutes, the pilot interrupted the silence by speaking over the internal comms system on the headset.

"You got ahold of DeKlerk's satellite phone and impersonated Balthazar to get me out here for a medevac?" the pilot said, putting the pieces together.

"You got it, pal. Found the phone and his maps in his pack."

A pause.

"Where are they?"

"The hunting party?"

"Yeah."

The American looked over at him.

"You might want to cancel their dinner reservations, my dude."

"Fuck."

"Yeah, exactly that. Listen, I know we're somewhere in Benin. I need you to fly me back to Niger."

"We don't have enough fuel."

"So we'll refuel. You have base camp that you've been operating these helicopters out of, where you've been running logistics out of."

The pilot swallowed.

"Yes, we have a base camp."

"Fly us there, you refuel, and we take back off. You talk to no one. You signal any type of distress to anyone at the camp, and I promise that you will die first."

The pilot swallowed again, then tilted the stick and turned them toward the base camp.

"We're also getting the other American out of there."

CHAPTER

53

Half an hour later the Sikorsky helicopter blasted over the treetops, and the hunting base camp came into view. Lopez was surprised. It was an impressive setup. They had erected some huge tents, it looked like a grill was set up, and of course there was a landing area for helicopters. Porters and security personnel milled about the camp below.

"Set the bird down right next to the fuel point," Lopez said before reminding the pilot, "Don't even think about playing fuck-around with me."

On the way in, he'd had the pilot radio to the base camp updating them on the situation. The new cover story was that De Klerk was stable; he just had a flesh wound. They were ferrying the body of the dead Ranger and were to bring Wallaby to the helipad so they could both be transferred over to the Russians in order to collect their bounty.

The pilot hesitated for a moment, clearly scared shitless by the whole scenario that was playing out before his eyes today. Lopez was unmoved. If Nick wanted to know what fear really felt like, he could try walking the previous day in his shoes. If not the previous week.

Tree branches swayed, and anything not tied down nearby went flying, including bits of trash, someone's suitcase, and a blue tarp someone left out. The aircraft rocked gently as it touched down and the pilot throttled down the engine.

Just outside the door were a half dozen fifty-five-gallon fuel drums, one of them sporting a real-deal gas pump affixed to the top, which was kept running by a small generator twenty meters away and linked with an extension cord.

Lopez motioned to the pilot with his Glock, and he got out to begin fueling up the bird.

Meanwhile, Lopez had put DeKlerk's hat back on and pulled the brim down over his face in case anyone got curious as to what exactly was going on at the fuel point. So far, no one seemed to suspect a thing. There were both white and black people in the camp, probably a combination of locally hired laborers and security contractors brought in from abroad.

He estimated that there were about two dozen of them in the camp, and he didn't relish getting into a firefight with them with his half-empty Glock. A few more minutes, and hopefully they would be able to make a clean exit with no one being the wiser.

Keeping a close eye on the pilot as he stood there filling the tank, Lopez made sure he didn't try to alert anyone. If this thing went pear shaped, he was screwed and knew it. He was a Ranger, not a helicopter pilot.

After several agonizing minutes, the pilot placed the spigot down on top of the fuel drum and climbed back into the helicopter.

Lopez squinted through the cockpit windshield as the pilot messed with the controls and prepared to take off.

"What. The. Fuck," Lopez said just loud enough for the pilot to hear him. "Is. She. Doing. Here?"

The pilot looked forward to see what his captor was talking about.

"Shit," he cursed. "She's coming to see you . . . well, I mean, she is coming to see DeKlerk. You reported him injured, after all."

"Get us the fuck out of here now."

The pilot began throttling up the engine way too late.

The side door on the Sikorsky slid open and Cassandra hopped in with Wallaby, who had his hands flex-cuffed behind him, sliding the door shut behind her.

She must have gotten ahold of one of the headsets back there, because suddenly her South African accent came over the internal comms.

"Koos, are you okay? They said you were injured."

Lopez stared wide-eyed at the pilot and mouthed two words.

Take. Off.

CHAPTER

54

LOPEZ UNBUCKLED HIS seat belt, took off his headset, and climbed into the back cab of the helicopter as they lifted off.

"Koos!" he heard her say again over the rotor blades. Then Lopez sat across from her and took his hat off.

Cassandra's eyes went crazy, then darted back and forth looking for a way out, but it was already too late. They were airborne and on their way to the border with Niger. Wallaby also looked up in recognition, seeing Lopez. He immediately jetted out of his seat and headbutted Cassandra.

She wrenched backward, her head bouncing off the side of the helicopter as she screamed obscenities. Lopez reached out and grabbed Wallaby, forcing him to sit down before he tried to eat one of her ears or her eyeballs in a moment of rage. Not that he wasn't sympathetic.

"Calm the fuck down," he yelled at the Task Force Orange operator as the helicopter jostled back and forth with the party going on in the cab. He pulled a small blade and cut the flex-cuffs off his teammate.

"What the hell is going on?" Wallaby asked.

"Pull on a headset."

Lopez pulled one of the headsets over his ears and threw another headset to Cassandra, who was rapidly developing a black eye. She and Wallaby both put their headsets on, and Lopez spoke into the mic.

"Long time no hear," Lopez said. "You've been ghosting me since our first date."

"Where is my uncle?"

"*Your uncle?*"

"Where is Koos?"

"Dead," Lopez reported emotionlessly.

Tears welled in the young woman's eyes, her cheeks glowing red with anger.

"You bastard."

"Honey, you slipped a Mickey in my drink and shanghaied me across an international border in order for a group of fucking psychopathic whack jobs to hunt me like an animal for sport. You're like some kind of fucked-up version of Charlize Theron."

"She did the same to me," Wallaby complained. "I got fucked, and not in a good way."

"But how was the food in the camp?"

"Oh, pretty good, actually," Wallaby said. "We barbecued some wild boar and—"

"We were hired to do a job, and we did it," Cassandra said, interrupting the banter. "Same as you."

"No, nothing like me. I kill to survive, not for petty vanity."

"That was the wealthy foreigners. My uncle wasn't one of them."

"Sure acted like them, though."

"We did a lot of bad things," she conceded. "But we too did those things to survive, as did you."

Lopez rubbed the week-old beard on his chin.

"Not buying it."

Cassandra sniffled, her bloodshot eyes staring daggers into him.

"The Russians wanted both of you gone. You were making trouble for them in Niger."

"So I hear."

"Their private military company, the Wagner Group, knew of my uncle's reputation as a mercenary on the continent and approached him for the job. 'Make these guys Lopez and Willoughby working out of the embassy in Niamey disappear.'"

"As fucked up as the Russians are, they usually just shoot you in the back of the head and call it good. You took it a bit further than that."

"Koos had been leading safaris off and on for years, taking wealthy people big-game hunting. Some of those wealthy people wanted a greater challenge, and so he took them to game preserves, but instead of hunting animals, they hunted the poachers there that were illegally killing the elephants."

"Nice business plan."

"But those wealthy Americans, they always wanted something more. They see themselves as society's real predators, feasting on the souls of the population of entire countries. They wanted to hunt a fellow predator to prove their prowess."

"So your uncle Koos connected A and B. He gets paid twice for doing one job."

"Good business sense."

Lopez rolled his eyes.

"You're heading back to Niger, yeah?"

"And without the benefits of a passport."

"You know who has been waiting several days to collect our remains at the border?"

"What?"

"The two Wagner commanders in Niger. Koos and I were to bring your body to them for confirmation and then collect the rest of our fee."

"You've gotta be shitting me," he said, but not surprised.

"Good luck, Lopez," Cassandra said. "You turned out to be dangerous game indeed."

With that, she reached for and slid open the side door. Wind rushed into the cab, blowing their hair back. Lopez lunged toward her just a second too late. Cassandra hurled herself out into the void and disappeared from view. Wallaby's jaw hung open, unable to talk, unsure what to do.

Lopez looked down but couldn't spot her. They were at least a thousand feet above the ground.

"Holy smokes."

The Ranger slid the door shut and climbed back into the shotgun seat in the cockpit.

"What the fuck is going on back there?" the pilot screamed at him.

Lopez pulled the headset back over his ears and leaned back in his seat.

"She pulled a brodie."

CHAPTER 55

LOPEZ DIRECTED THE pilot to drop altitude and circle back around. No one survived a fall like that, but for some reason he still felt like he needed to see it for himself.

A few minutes and several passes later, he located Cassandra's remains lying in a flat open area. Lopez turned away and told the pilot to continue on their course toward Niger.

He would not have killed an unarmed woman in cold blood, but apparently she didn't know that and, seeing no way out of her predicament, had chosen her own way to check out. Considering her treatment toward him, Lopez didn't know why he felt shitty about the whole situation, but he did.

He was still trying to get over the shock of it. Wallaby, on the other hand, seemed satisfied enough with the outcome.

His mind went mostly blank as he stared out through the windshield for the better part of an hour as the savannah below screamed by and eventually thinned out into the Sahel, which seemed to stretch out into infinity in all directions.

The pilot spotted the trucks first. He pointed through the window to draw Lopez's attention to two Toyota pickups parked in the middle of the expanse of the Sahel. Lopez instructed the pilot to land a few hundred meters away from the Wagner mercenaries.

"Keep the engine going," Lopez told him as they landed. "Take off as soon as I'm out."

"You're just going to let me go?" the pilot asked, trying to keep the tremble out of his voice.

Lopez glared over at him.

"Consider a new line of work," he said. "And I don't mean being a helicopter pilot."

The pilot simply nodded as he landed the bird, and Lopez hopped out, pulling DeKlerk's hat over his head again and holding it in place against the beating rotor blades.

The resulting wind blew at Lopez's tattered clothing as the helicopter lifted off and headed back the way it had come. Sliding open the door to the cab, he helped Wallaby out of the helicopter. Wallaby kept his hands clasped behind his back as if he were still captive.

Lopez pulled the brim of DeKlerk's hat over his face as he began walking toward the vehicles.

As he approached, the Russians began calling out to him in English, which must have been the common language between them and the South African.

"Where the hell have you been?" one of them slurred in a thick Russian accent.

"Where is the corpse of the Ranger?" the other shouted. "We heard he was dead."

Lopez kept his head down and closed the distance.

"No body, no payment. It's that simple," the other said.

When he was within ten feet, Lopez looked up to get a better look at the two Russian mercenaries. Far from the portrayal of mercenaries in the movies, these guys looked like diabetic alcoholics, with fat bellies and wrinkled skin that made middle-aged men look like nursing home candidates.

"DeKlerk, do you fucking hear me?" one of them shouted.

Then the other. "Wait, who the fuck are—"

Lopez reached for the hat with his nondominant hand, took it off his head, and let it fall to the hard-packed sand at their feet.

The two men stared at Lopez for a long, pregnant pause that seemed to linger in the air. Lopez stared right back at them.

Then he leveled his Glock 19 on the closest Wagner mercenary and squeezed the trigger, sending a single 9mm round punching through his forehead and giving him a third eye. He collapsed, down and out.

The second mercenary reached for a Makarov pistol in his waistband but was far too slow. Lopez transitioned from his first target to the second and squeezed off two shots center mass, putting them through the Russian's chest and then following up with a third shot that took him in the face. He fell like a marionette that had its strings suddenly cut.

Lopez holstered his pistol and knelt down to begin rifling through the pockets of the two dead bodies. Wallaby used the opportunity to arm himself with the dead men's weapons.

Each of the Russians had the key to their own vehicle. Lopez chose the one that had the most gas in the tank when he started them up, then climbed in and got behind the wheel as Wallaby got into the passenger seat.

Reversing and spinning the wheel in a cloud of dust, Lopez braked and put the pickup into drive and gunned it down the rural dirt road that led north.

He left nothing behind him but expended brass and dead bodies.

EPILOGUE

"SIT THE FUCK down right there," one of the JSOC officers ordered Lopez.

He winced as he sat down on one of the office chairs. They were in one of the large open work areas in the embassy, where most days a small group of analysts and officers from the Defense Intelligence Agency would be busy typing up cable traffic to send back to the States.

Now the office was largely vacant due to the protests outside the embassy gates. The muted chants and screams could even be heard inside the office.

Lopez had a bandage on the side of his head, he wore a sling (his shoulder had been partially dislocated without him realizing it), and his body was covered in bruises and contusions, not to mention that he was feeling the effects of food and sleep deprivation as well as dehydration.

He'd been back in Niamey only twenty-four hours, but the embassy's physician assistant had done a good job getting him patched up and made some follow-up doctor appointments for him in the States.

The JSOC crew at the embassy had not been so kind, however. They had been grilling him and Wallaby separately. Again.

"How long do we got?" the JSOC officer asked one of the DIA staffers.

"Marines flying in sometime in the next forty-eight to begin the NEO," the DIA staffer said. Lopez knew that meant a noncombatant evacuation operation, or an embassy evacuation.

According to the intel, the Russian Wagner Group had paid off Nigerien military officers to stage a coup during the time that he was in Benin. This was followed up by a Russian disinformation operation run on Nigerien social media, stoking tensions and getting anti-American protesters out in the streets. No wonder they had wanted him out of their hair when they were launching such a bold action.

Lopez had told his story, and it certainly made sense, given the context that the Russians would want America's recce guy working out of the embassy taken out of the game beforehand. But his words had fallen on the dead ears of skeptical officers.

The JSOC officer turned around and walked back to Lopez.

"When the Marines get here, you are on the first fucking thing smoking out of this country and back to Benning, where you are going to be nailed to a fucking cross. Never in my entire career have I come across a sergeant as unprofessional as you."

"Sir, I—"

"Don't *sir* me, motherfucker. You went AWOL for almost two weeks, out there getting your ashes hauled by the local gals and knocking back cold ones, and when you sobered up you dragged yourself back here with the most asinine story any of us have ever heard. I just got off the red line with JSOC. They want your scalp, the commander of the 75th wants your scalp, special ops command wants your scalp. You're fucked. You're fucking done, Sergeant, a rank you won't be holding for much longer."

Lopez opened his mouth to say something but thought better of it. He got up out of his chair and waddled over to the coffeemaker on swollen, blistered feet. The Ranger poured some of the black sludge into a Styrofoam cup.

"Hey, you seeing this?" the DIA guy shouted from across the office. He was pointing to the large flat-screen television mounted on the wall.

The JSOC officer walked over, grabbed the remote control off a desk, and turned up the volume. A blonde news anchor from one of the twenty-four-hour news channels was speaking from their studio in New York.

"Getting reports in now, this is breaking news, we're going to keep following this and bring you any updates." The anchor paused for a moment, apparently listening to something being said in her earpiece. "Sorry, folks, this is all coming in to us, and we're giving it to you in real time." Another pause.

"Okay, we're being told that the Belgian royal family was killed just days ago during a hunting safari in the West African country of Benin."

The JSOC officer turned to look at Lopez, who shrugged in return as he drank his coffee. Lopez was in full don't-give-a-fuck mode at this point. The JSOC officer had it out for him, but Wallaby would be able to confirm the most salient parts of his story.

"All right, it seems that there was another hunting accident in Benin around the same time. We're unclear on whether these events are connected. I'm being told now that a group of wealthy American businessmen have also been reported killed during a similar safari. We're getting some of the names of the deceased, we'll have to confirm them, but we're being told that tech billionaire Balthazar Botha, the owner of Titan Rockets and car manufacturer Taggart, is among the dead. Also, Henry Williamsburg III, owner of the world's largest social media—"

The JSOC officer hit the mute button on the television set and walked over to Lopez, who by now had a shit-eating grin on his face.

He spun Lopez around in the office swivel chair and grasped him by both shoulders.

"You will return to Fort Benning on the first American aircraft out of this country. You will report directly to your regimental commander," the JSOC officer said, their faces just inches apart, his voice practically a whisper. "And you will say absolutely nothing about any of this to anyone, ever."

"Yes, sir."

The JSOC officer went back to the television and turned the volume back on.

"—already being called the largest hunting accident of its kind. It is unclear if the hunting parties ran into Islamic militants that are known to be active in the northern parts of Benin or possibly armed poachers."

Lopez stood and finished the rest of his coffee, threw the cup in the trash, and walked out of the office.

He had bags to pack, then maybe one last drink at the Raddison before America dipped out on yet another of its military commitments and shipped him back to Georgia.

ACKNOWLEDGMENTS

PUBLISHED JUST OVER a century ago, *The Most Dangerous Game* by Richard Connell continues to inspire writers like me all these years later. The short story's countless adaptions (my favorite is the film *Surviving the Game*, starring Ice-T and Rutger Hauer) now include *The Most Dangerous Man*, which puts a modern twist on the age-old story.

I would also like to acknowledge another short story that appears in this work, *The Ghost Lemurs of Madagascar* by William Burroughs. Sometimes referred to as Burroughs's *Necronomicon*, it does indeed fit nicely within the cosmic dread authored by H. P. Lovecraft. But Burroughs settles on a horror even more terrifying than the Elder Gods, that being the annihilation of time itself. This work is cited by various occultists, philosophers, and magicians, and it fits well in this story—and into a world where artificial intelligence promises us a utopian future. But is it a false prophet? Time will tell.

A shout-out to two other literary influences: First is Don Pendleton, who authored the Mack Bolan novels I grew up reading as a teenager and who coined the term "action-adventure." The second author who inspired me and so many others is the titan of adventure himself, Robert E. Howard, whose Conan stories leap right off the page. I am merely following in the footsteps of Pendleton and Howard, hoping that I don't let them down.

My editor Tom Wickersham was of invaluable assistance during the writing of this book. I had never worked with an editor on fictional works, and although I was cautious about such an endeavor, the arrangement paid off in spades. I hope he's as happy with this novel as I am. His suggestions helped shape the plot of *The Most Dangerous Man* in critical ways.

My agent, Alec Shane, is greatly appreciated. He tried to meddle with my copy several times, but I still like the guy and found his assistance on the publishing and business side of this industry to be a huge help.

Other authors and friends have supported me and offered me advice, enough that it's impossible to mention them all, and the secret squirrels who still work for the government wouldn't want me publishing their names anyway. A few authors whose support is greatly appreciated are I. S. Berry, Chuck Rogers, Ivan Ingraham, Steven Hildreth, Mark Greaney, and Joshua Hood. I'm also grateful to work with our Team House podcast producer, Dee Kontakos, and my journalistic colleague at the High Side, Sean Naylor, whose support and friendship mean a lot to me.

I would also like to thank Alice and Kasiet, both of whom have supported me and kept me from going off the rails in more ways than they will ever know.